ABOUT THE AUTHOR

Brian Jarman was born on a farm in Mid-Wales, the joint youngest of five brothers. After studying in London, Paris and Cardiff, he joined the South Wales Argus as a reporter and then worked for the BBC for 22 years, mainly as a current affairs editor for the World Service. For the past ten years he was Senior Editor, Journalism at London Metropolitan University. He's published four other novels: **The Missing Room, The Fall from Howling Hill, The Final Trick** and **The Absent Friend**. He's set up a literary consultancy, helpmepublish.co.uk.

Published by Fitzrovia Books, London

Copyright © 2020 by Brian Jarman

2nd edition

ISBN: 9798683402501

REVIEWS

SATURDAYS ARE BLACK or WHITE

It's real and emotional. It's funny and alive. Self-reflective, preceptive, literary, affectionate, witty - all that.
Victoria Neumark Jones, literary journalist and lecturer

THE FINAL TRICK

What I liked best about it, apart from the storytelling talents - always so good - was the personality of the narrator. Everything is alive in this novel, and the plot and atmosphere vvvvv good.
Carmen Callil, founder of Virago Press

THE MISSING ROOM

An ingenious page turner, but with the power to encourage reflection on the human condition. It's all there: family, health, career, and of course the slippery slope to alcoholism.

Clive Jennings, Director of the National Print Gallery

AUTHOR'S ACKNOWLEDGEMENTS

Mega thanks as always go to my editor Annabel Hughes for her forensic proof-reading and insightful suggestions. I'm also grateful to the members of my family who gave me their support and encouragement, and to Victoria Neumark Jones and Phil Jones for being so nice about it.

This book is dedicated to the memory of Iris Jarman, and to her daughters Paula, Tricia and Trudy.

To: Tristram

Fellow Fitzrovian & Celt

Brian

August 22

SATURDAYS ARE BLACK OR WHITE

By Brian Jarman

1 **Saturdays are black**

'Hullo. It's me. I haven't got long. Cancer. Thought you'd like to know.'

That was it. No goodbye or anything. No 'Get in touch.' The beep signalled the end of the message, and the machine whirred and clicked, ready to receive more.

Arwyn slumped down into his old leather armchair and stared out of the window into Marylebone Lane. It was early evening, and people were rushing from work or shopping, popping into the patisserie or wine shop opposite to grab something on the way home. Satie's *Gymnopédie* was playing on the radio, which had always evoked for him a languid afternoon, with just the vaguest undertone of trouble to come.

He'd recognised the voice straightaway, of course, at the hello, although he hadn't heard it for.......what? Must be getting on for thirty years now. He cast his mind back to when they'd last seen each other. Surely it was at their fiftieth birthday party. He'd organised it all: the jazz band and the hog roast at The Dragon in Cwmbach, in the garden by the stream. Did they fall out then? Or was it more a question of drifting apart, of irreconcilable differences?

He hauled himself up and went through to the kitchen where he took down his favourite cut glass tumbler from the cupboard, and from the freezer fished out ice cubes and the lime wedges he kept there for the purpose - quartered then halved again. It was a little early, but what the hell - he'd had a bit of a shock. He threw a handful of ice into the glass, then a healthy slug of vodka, savouring the crackle as he did so. He went to screw the cap back on the bottle, but poured in a little more for good measure. He filled the glass almost to the brim with slimline tonic, plonked in two lime eighths, swirled it around, and took a huge gulp. It was important to do things in the right order.

He went back into the living room and replayed the message. No new information. No tone or inflection to give him a clue as to the speaker's frame of mind, or intention. It was calm, measured, neutral.

He sat down again and pondered why Bren thought he would like to know. Twins are often supposed to be able to read each other's thoughts, or feel each other's pain, but they never had, or wanted to.

Yes, in a certain sense they could predict what the other would say or do in a given circumstance, but this was more in the mould of an old married couple rather than any telepathic power. In the days when they were actually speaking to each other, that is.

When they were young Arwyn would sometimes catch their mother telling a friend that they did indeed have this gift.

'The other day,' she would be saying, 'Bren came into the kitchen and asked a question. Five minutes later, Arwyn came in and asked the very same question.'

'But Mam, what was the question?' he would ask.

'Well - what's for tea?' their mother would be forced to admit, but not for a moment allowing this to shake her theory. For some reason, when he pictured this scene now, he focused on a corner of the coffee table in the farmhouse living room that had been broken off. Their mother was never one for squandering money on new furniture when perfectly good stuff was handed down in the family, or she'd picked something up at the periodic auctions she liked going to down in Abergavenny.

Yet the family myth of their secret communication persisted. They'd had a sort of den in an old henhouse in the field below the farm. After much debate, the twins called it simply The Den - they couldn't agree on anything else. One day his father announced that he needed the henhouse and they'd have to clear their stuff out. For some reason, he allowed them to keep just four things and the rest would be burnt. He'd told them this separately. Apparently they named exactly the same items - he couldn't recall them all now, but he thought there was an old school desk, and a Noddy alarm clock, with Noddy's head nodding as it ticked. But the truth of it, as far as Arwyn was concerned, was that the rest of their stuff was rubbish, and he was glad to see the back of it.

What, he now wondered, was behind Bren's call? Did he want something - a phone call or even a visit -

or was he saying that Arwyn should get himself checked out, being identical twins and all? Cancer was not something that was common in the Fflints - in fact it was virtually unknown. They were long livers. It was cardiovascular problems that often carried them off, eventually. There was a recognised fondness of the bottle in the males, although drive and ambition saved them from outright alcoholism. It was known in the family as the Fflint Inheritance. Legend had it that Great Uncle Ted had been feeling distinctly unwell and so paid a rare visit to the doctor's, probably at about the same age as Arwyn was now.

'You're drinking yourself to a slow death,' was the diagnosis.

'Oh, don't worry, Doc,' said Ted. 'I'm in no hurry.' The Fflints had always had a down-to-earth approach to death. While they did not exactly go gentle into that good night, as their national poet warned against, they didn't want to make too much of a fuss either.

And knees. The Fflints suffered from weak knees in later life.

But cancer? At this age? In their family? It was difficult to swallow. Arwyn supposed he'd have to make an appointment at the doctor's - he was no keener than Great Uncle Ted on a visit. But that could take time, and there was the question of whether he should go to see his brother first. He didn't even know what type of cancer it was. Beyond this, though, he had no idea whether or not there would be a welcome, and shrank from the possibility that there would be none. Theirs had always been a rather odd relationship, intense but not at all twinny.

He flicked through his mental photo album of their childhood. They'd been inseparable, but this was hardly surprising as they were each other's sole soulmates on the remote farm in the Black Mountains. Their brother Will was much older and had his own life and family.

The twins ran free, built dens in the woods, fished in the Bechan brook and looked for mischief. There was farm and school work too as they grew older, but they were energetic, spirited and bright.

They were also great rivals. Everything was a competition. Their father Dai, a man of few words, was intolerant of this. When they were six or seven their mother was serving up fish and chips for dinner. Arwyn stared down at his plate.

'Mam, Bren's got twelve chips and I've only got eleven.'

His father's arm reached out from his place at the end of the table and give his earlobe a hard twist. You weren't meant to complain about the food that was put in front of you. The tweak hurt, and thereafter Arwyn was more careful around their father.

Nell was more accommodating towards her sons' intense rivalries and had developed strategies to manage them. There was the principle of 'one cut and one choose': if they were given an apple to share, one would cut it in half and the other would have first pick, and neither could complain. The cutter would perform the procedure with all the precision of a surgeon to make sure that the chooser could not get one atom more of apple.

They competed for her love, too. When they climbed up beside her on the settee before bedtime for a cwtch, one of them would trace a line down her face with his finger, the other watching hawk-eyed for any deviation. They were only allowed to kiss their own side of the face.

Arwyn once asked Nell to tell him, honestly, which of them she loved the most.

'Whoever needs me most at the time,' said Nell in her no-nonsense way, busy with some mysterious ritual in the kitchen.

Then there was this weird thing about counting. Numbers seemed to creep into almost every argument they had. They had a system called The Finish of the Count.

I love Mam more than you do.
I love her a million.
I love her a billion.
A trillion.
A gazillion.
A gazillion and one.
A gazillion and two.
I love her to the Finish of the Count.
I love her to the Finish of the Count plus one.

There would then be a brief interlude of debate about whether there could ever be one over the Finish of the Count. This was never settled satisfactorily, but the losing side at that point would seize the advantage and plunge in.

The Finish of the Count plus a million.

The Finish of the Count plus a million and one.

Plus a billion.

Plus a billion and one

Plus a trillion.

And so it went on. They even argued about who would live the longest. Bren was twenty minutes older, so Arwyn used to taunt him that he would go first. He now remembered his mother telling him that the matron at the hospital told her that Bren would always struggle, because he pushed his way out first, whereas Arwyn simply slipped out in his wake. He supposed Bren had had the harder life - farming is not an easy life. And then there was Jac, of course.....

But over time it was Bren who clung more to Nell, and Arwyn accepted this extra closeness with equanimity for he was already eyeing distant horizons. There was the question of what the boys would do after school. Both were 'book smart' as their father said, and worked hard at their A levels. Arwyn was dreaming of foreign travel and applied to university in London to study international relations. He'd written off for details about the Foreign Office and what was needed to apply. Secretly, he harboured ambitions of becoming a spy.

Bren had set his sights on agricultural college in Aberystwyth and intended to stay farming with Dai and Will. Although there was enough work and living for the four of them, Arwyn could see that increasing mechanisation was cutting the need for manpower. He reasoned to himself that he could leave the homestead with good conscience because his father and brothers would do very well, better even, without him. All this was endorsed by the family without much discussion. At that time, in that part of the world, undergraduates usually got paid full grants covering both tuition fees and living expenses, so it would cost neither him nor his parents a penny.

When the day came for him to leave, his mother as usual coped with her distress by busying herself with detail. She'd bought an old trunk for him at an auction and he caught her slipping in such essentials as tea and toilet rolls.

'They have those things in London, Mam.'

'Ah well, better to be safe than sorry,' she said.

Before he climbed into the Land Rover for the drive down to Abergavenny station with his father, she hugged him with a tear in her eye but otherwise no fuss. Bren was off working in the upper fields some-where, so as far as Arwyn could recall, the two never said goodbye. There was, deep down, a sense of sad-ness at leaving his double, his constant companion since birth and even before, but this was largely over-ridden by his sense of wonder at this embarkation to undiscovered worlds, and of being one of a kind in-stead of one of a pair. He'd long resented being bun-dled together with his brother as if he were just half of a unit. Even when asked the simple question 'Where's Bren?' he would bridle and grunt: 'How should I know?' How glorious it would be to arrive in the big city being a person in his own right, just one of him.

He took to London as if it were the one place he was meant to be. He did well enough at university, still planning on joining the Foreign Office. But at the bot-tom of one of his essays, his tutor wrote: 'You may not have the deepest penetration into the subject, but you can lay it out so clearly. Have you ever thought of becoming a journalist?'

He'd always remembered her words, for they set him on his career. He had never given any thought to jour-nalism, although looking back there were some signs.

He and Bren had set up a newspaper when they were about thirteen or so, writing out all the local and family news and circulating it to interested parties. It didn't last all that long, for there were so many other demands on their time.

He went to see the university's careers officer.

'Forget it,' he said. 'It's competitive and the quality nationals still like taking graduates from Ox- ford and Cambridge. You'd probably have to start on a local paper, covering parish councils and the opening of fetes.'

It was a challenge that Arwyn eagerly took up. He quite liked the idea of being a professional nosey parker chronicling all facets of life, big and small. He involved himself in student journalism, becoming editor of the University of London newspaper which had a good reputation. Much to his surprise, he got a job straight from graduation on the Western Chronicle in Cardiff. They tested their cub reporters, as they called them, by sending them to the shittiest jobs, the most dreaded of which was the death knock. When routine calls to the police revealed an interesting death, the cubs were immediately sent out to get the story and the pics. The cubs got used to doors being slammed angrily in their face, and Arwyn for one understood why. But you never knew how people were going to react.

He'd particularly dreaded going to the house of a seventeen-year-old on a council estate somewhere in the mining valleys - the kind where there were cars on bricks and old cookers in the front garden. The woman who came to the door looked worn out and had red eyes. When he explained who he was she more or less yanked him inside, sat him down, gave him tea and biscuits and started telling him how wonderful her son was. She called his Nan over from across the street so she could have her say. When he asked for a photo of him, she brought out a huge album and started taking him through it.

'There, wasn't he the cutest baby you ever saw?' Arwyn tried to explain that he was on a deadline and had to leave so it could make that evening's paper, but the mother pressed on undeterred. She wanted her son to have a good write-up. Then she took him into the kitchen to show him the stove. It was leaking fumes, she said, and making them all ill. He said she'd have to take it up with the council, but she said they weren't interested. He felt sorry for her, but at least the story made the front page.

After three or four years on the beat, he was made a very young Foreign Correspondent on a Fleet Street daily. His dream of travel and adventure had been realised. This led a few years later to his own television programme, *In Like Flint*, a weekly investigation into a topic of the day, both at home and abroad. He'd always hated the title, and its anglicisation. He'd argued with the producers that it should be changed to Fflint and explained in vain that in Welsh one f is pronounced as a v, and that's why it needed two. But it caught on and stuck.

With all the deadlines and the travel, he had excuses for not going back to Cwmbach more often than he wanted to. He was always expected back for Christmas, which he could usually plan for, and a couple of weekends or family occasions throughout the year. He enjoyed going there in a way, as a kind of reality check for he still had a deep fondness and respect for his family. But his visits were both a source of joy, in seeing old familiar faces and places, and sorrow, that the folks back home seemed content to trundle along at the same old pace without any ambition to experience more of life. He was always eager to return to London.

By then he and Bren had developed a sort of taciturn politeness with one another, both aware that they now moved in different and distinct worlds, ploughing their own furrows. Much of the old rivalry seemed to have burnt itself out and Arwyn liked to believe that both were enjoying their new-found lives as individuals. Somewhere at the back of everything though, there was a watching, an evaluating, a judging of who was doing better in life, who was happier, who would make their mother the most proud.

After all this rambling that Saturday evening, Arwyn groped for that original question that was still niggling at the back of his mind. He realised like a time-elapsed video that he was now on his third rather large V&T. He couldn't take it like he used to, naturally, but somehow, when he was in the mood, old habits fought for life and refused to go quietly.

Yes, that question - why did he and Bren stop speaking all those years ago? Their communication up until then had been, at best, sporadic: Arwyn spend much of his time travelling or working to tight production schedules, and it was hard for Bren's to get away from the farm. He rarely came up to London - once or twice to the Smithfield Show when he would stay in Arwyn's flat of the time. They would make family small talk, catching up in a desultory way, each preferring to be with his own ilk.

The idea for the joint fiftieth party must have come from someone else. Neither one of them would have contemplated the prospect for a moment. Arwyn rather fancied it was Bren's wife Meryl who suddenly broached the subject the Christmas before.

'But of course you're going to have to have a party. The family expects. You know they like a good do.'

Alwyn's initial inner response was: 'Well, they can whistle.' Bren, though, always a stickler for family convention, joined forces with Meryl - somewhat uncharacteristically in Arwyn's view.

'We should, really,' Bren had said.

In then end, Arwyn organised the whole thing, which was how he liked it. In his job he'd become quite good at getting things done, and considered Bren's approach more laissez-faire, shall we say? Used to modern London ways and arranging international travel at a moment's notice, he was somewhat sur-

prised when he rang a local bus company to book the trans-
port from the farm to the pub.

'Right, that's in the book for May 1st,' said the gruff
voice on the end of the line.

'Don't you want a deposit or anything'?

'Nah, cash on the day will be fine.'

'Well, can I take the driver's mobile in case there's a
last minute hitch?'

'Don't know who it'll be yet. He probably hasn't got
one.'

Arwyn was forgetting that mobile phone's were still
the accessory of the elite. A couple of weeks before
when they were making plans for the party, he'd rang
Bren in a taxi on the way home from work.

'Are you in a taxi?' asked Bren. Taxis were considered an extravagance in Cwmbach.

'On a mobile phone?' Arwyn admitted this was the
case.

'You bloody yuppie,' said Bren. Arwyn did not point
out that the y stood for young.

What he was yet to discover was that Annie, Bren's
former girlfriend whom he'd chucked over to marry
Meryl, had a link with The Dragon. Her son Eifion
was the manager. Over the phone he was friendly but

also professionalism personified in a way that Arwyn had forgotten persisted. He would recognise the name of Fflint for sure.

'Jazz band? I'll send you a list of the ones we've used. Best are from Brecon, if you can get 'em. Hog roast? The people up at The Hall do those. Supply the local butchers, they do. None better.'

When the estimate arrived Arwyn thought there must be some mistake. Surely it couldn't be that cheap? In the next phone call he tried as casually as he could to confirm the price. It was duly confirmed. Arwyn accepted it graciously but made a mental note to give Eifion a good tip at the end of it all.

Bren had also put him in charge of the guest list - all the family and neighbours. By the time Arwyn put two and two together and worked out that Eifion must be Annie's son, he decided that he would have to invite her too. They'd kept in touch, off and on. He'd always been fond of her and couldn't simply switch off his affection when Bren called it off, even though Bren had seemed to expect him to. So he invited Annie to the party at The Dragon.

It started off auspiciously. It was a sunny day, the driver turned up bang on time, and Eifion had done

exactly as he'd been asked. The twins were greeted by the jazz band in waistcoats of many colours. The lead sax player said, 'So you're a hundred years old?'
'That's right,' they said.

'Let me guess. You're forty,' he said to Arwyn, 'and he's sixty.'
Both twins laughed.

They played their favourites: *The A Train, Blueberry Hill, Stranger on the Shore*. Things went swimmingly until it came time to cut the cake. Annie came in wielding a large knife at shoulder height as if to stab someone and made to lunge at Bren. Gasps ran around the room. She said afterwards that it was a joke - she'd always had a sense of fun and mischief - but Meryl took great exception to it, and the fact that Annie had been invited in the first place. After that, Arwyn had to admit to himself, things became a little blurred, but he suspected various old sores were re-opened on both sides.

Weeks went by without communication between the brothers, then months, then years. So while the party was the tipping point, Arwyn would even now be hard pushed to pinpoint with any degree of accuracy the

resentments that lay at the bottom of their estrangement.

Maybe he didn't want to dig up the past. He'd come
to no conclusion about what he should now do, if anything. It was Sunday tomorrow, so no doctor's appointment could be made until Monday. He saw he
should make some response to the phone message, as
terse as it was, but he couldn't see what. Maybe things
would be clearer tomorrow.

He had an uneasy night, broken by one of his old
work dreams. He was in Bosnia, during the war. His
producer rang from London saying they were doing a
special programme and he would be on air in an hour.
He had no production crew, no interview material and
no script. In the next moment, he was in a studio with
new digital equipment which he didn't know how to
use. There were a couple of people in the shadows but
they took no notice of his appeals for help. The clock
was ticking to his deadline. He had no idea what to
do.

2.Sundays are sandpaper

It was a warm autumn morning. What was the phrase - *season of mists and mellow fruitfulness*? Keats, wasn't it? Mortality and melancholy and all that. But Arwyn felt alive as he walked down Marylebone Lane and crossed a largely deserted Wigmore Street. He looked up as he did so towards the greyish haze of the trees in Portman Square. The view had the feel of an impressionist painting, one of Monet's haunting depictions of the Houses of Parliament, maybe. It was odd to think now that the term impressionist was originally a derogative term coined by an art critic: it was just an impression of something, rather than an accurate representation. But for generations, and for Arwyn, its artists had captured some deeper and more eternal truth than the bustle of the everyday.

This otherworldliness put him in a good frame of mind for the pleasures that awaited him - one of the occasional jaunts around the bars of Soho with Freddie, the son of a second (or was it third?) cousin and his godson.

He was going to be late and Freddie would be tight-lipped with his military aversion to bad timekeeping. Everything seemed to take Arwyn longer these days. He was losing his dexterity, yes, but it was more than that. His theory was that with age you became aware at some level that time was running out, and patience with it. You got very grumpy when you had to spend what seemed like hours waiting for your bank's helpline to answer, or even for those infuriating whirling circles on your computer to stop.

Just that morning he had reached for his shaving foam from the bathroom shelves and he must have hit them awkwardly for the whole thing came crashing down, flinging bottles and jars onto the floor and into the bath. When he saw the shelves lying on the floor, it came to him that Bren had made them as a kind of going away present all those years ago, although they would never have been given such a grand title. Bren had always been handy with his hands. He didn't have time to clear it up.

'More haste, less speed,' he thought. It had taken him years to understand the axiom, assuming there was some subtle difference between the two adjectives which was beyond him. One day it occurred to him that what it meant was the more you hurry, the longer it would take because things would go wrong. He knew that now only too well.

They'd always been close, he and Freddie, from the time he was tiny. Freddie had come to live with him and Diana for a few weeks when he was seventeen, after his father had chucked him out for leaving his weed paraphernalia all over the house. He ended up staying for three years. Arwyn had encouraged him to go to university. He was bright and had an engaging style of writing; he used to show him his journal and Arwyn thought he'd make a fine journalist. But Freddie was not of an academic frame of mind. He scraped through with one A level in Criminal Psychology and then took to his room, smoking some kind of strong illegal substance late into the night and sleeping most of the day. He spoke of mood swings and suicidal thoughts. Arwyn dragged him off to the doctor, praying it wouldn't be the awful Charlotte Davies who treated patients as if they were wasting her valuable time with trivialities. But she was the only one available. Freddie insisted that Arwyn came in with him. She fired off questions at Freddie as if he were in the dock on a serious charge. Freddie, though, could be impressively articulate when he wanted to and countered her cross-examination expertly. Even Arwyn could see that he was not coming across as a potential suicide. After a few minutes she gave an exasperated sigh and said she could arrange for sessions with a psychiatrist. As soon as they stepped out of the surgery Freddie announced he would not be going. By this time he had the idea of joining the army, and he was convinced this course of action would ruin his chances.

Things came to a bit of a head when Freddie went on holiday with his mates to Thailand and met the girl of his dreams, a student at Bristol University. He more or less moved her into the flat, much to Diana's annoyance. But Arwyn pointed out that she'd soon be going back to Bristol, and once she did she ignored all Freddie's advances - he'd bought her a ring and and said he would move to Bristol. But he heard nothing from her. He began to talk actively of doing away with himself.

Eventually Arwyn had had enough. He spoke to a psychotherapist friend of his and asked her advice how to handle it. She told him to call his bluff and ask him how he intended topping himself. It seemed a risky strategy, but Jilly told him to trust her. He did, and the next time he mentioned it Arwyn swallowed hard and enquired exactly how he planned to carry out his threat.

'Jump from your skylight window,' he said after a moment's hesitation.

'Please don't do that,' said Arwyn. 'Think of all the mess and hassle I'd have to deal with. Cops, doctors, inquests. What you need to do is put on your old army greatcoat, fill the pockets with big stones, and go and jump off Tower Bridge.'

'Right,' said Freddie, 'I will,' his mouth set in a grim line. Suicide was never mentioned again.

He did join the army and turned his life around. Now, Arwyn suspected, he was working for M15. It was naturally never acknowledged, and officially he was with the Foreign Office but Freddie had once told him that if ever he saw him on the tube, he should ignore him. The inference was that he would be following someone.

Freddie's M15 ambitions began when Arwyn introduced him to an old classmate of his, Dai the Spy. Dai, of course, denied that he was a spy and got annoyed if he heard anyone using the nickname. Proof, his friend would say, that he was in fact a spy. Dai maintained that he was an engineer working for the Foreign Office. He certainly knew about phone bugging, as Arwyn found out when he came home from filming in the Gulf War. He'd done a programme out there about Operation Desert Storm, and when he came back he did a follow-up about efforts to release the British and American hostages held in Iraqi jails. He'd interviewed the Junior Minister at the Foreign Office at the time, but only one short clip was included in the broadcast. This was his editor Miranda's decision, but fully endorsed by Arwyn. It was partly because the Junior Minister had nothing interesting or important to say - it was all just waffle - and partly because Arwyn had contact with some of the released hostages who were critical of the Foreign Office. One,

whom they filmed anonymously in black-out to pro-
tect his mates left behind, said 'Keep those Foreign
Office wankers off the air until they have something
new to say.' They'd bleeped out the wankers, of
course. The returnees had also been interviewed by
the Foreign Office, who seemed to believe that the returnees were giving Arwyn's programme extra information. In this, they were probably right.

The Foreign Office were furious when they saw the
programme. They rang Arwyn up demanding that a
full interview be broadcast. He passed the call on to
Miranda. She was a master in dealing with things like
that. She stuck to her guns and said no.

It was after this that Arwyn noticed odd sounds on
his phone. He told Miranda and she said the same
thing was happening to her. In conversation with Dai
the Spy, Arwyn asked casually how someone would
know if their phone was tapped. He said that when
you picked up the phone, there would be a couple of
clicks before the dialling tone started. Then there
would be a ding, usually late at night when they
stopped monitoring the calls. He listened carefully the
next time he made a call. There were the two clicks.
And the little ding at half past midnight. He compared

notes with Miranda - this was exactly what was happening to her. They thought about reporting it, and talked it over and over, but in the end came to the conclusion that they would get nowhere with it.

His occasional Sunday outings with Freddie followed the well-worn furrow ploughed in their younger, boozier days. While Arwyn was a little more temperate now, and to some extent Freddie was too, he found ways to simulate the sessions of the past, slipping a little water in his wine and nursing his drinks a little longer than he used to.

They started off in the French House in Dean Street, the headquarters of De Gaulle's Free French in the war and an oasis for such louche luminaries as Dylan Thomas of Gentle Night fame. With its wooden panelling, old black and white pictures and unchanging aura it was still a mecca for characters and eccentrics - men with floppy hats and women with swirling garb. One regular perched at the bar with a placid parrot perched on her shoulder: she was as colourfully dressed as it was.

Freddie used to admit in his wilderness days that if he went out on a crawl with his mates he would time his round so that it was at the French House, as they sold only half-pints of beer. Nowadays their ritual was to start off sharing a bottle of Cidre Breton, and when Arwyn pushed his way through the throng he found Freddie sitting at a corner table with the cider in front of him. With his short-cropped hair and Kitchener moustache, he was such a far cry from that lost boy in the attic all those years ago. When he moved in he was given the choice of the spare room or the sprawling attic above their flat. He chose the latter. As time went on, Arwyn had wanted him to move down to the spare room. He thought the change from his attic lair would help him make a new start. Freddie refused.

'It's every teenager's dream,' he'd said, sprawling down on the futon.

'But you're twenty-two,' Arwyn had said.

Freddie rose to greet him in mock formality.

'And who are Her Majesty's Secret Services keeping their eagle eyes on this week?' asked Arwyn, once he'd caught his breath after his stroll. Freddie of course never talked about his work - what spy would? But he went along with the banter, and Arwyn was never one hundred per cent sure that he wasn't been strung along on some elaborate hoax.

'If I told you I'd have to slip a Mickey Finn into your cider unobserved,' said Freddie, raising his glass. 'But then, what would a humble road sweeper know about such matters?'

When Freddie had first started talking about applying to M15, he came up with the codeword road sweeper: if his nearest and dearest asked him what his job was and he said that, they would know he had indeed joined.

'Well, how are the roads then?'

'Busy. Dirty.'

After the French House they walked around the corner to The Coach and Horses, another throwback and erstwhile haunt of the notoriously hell-raising hack, Jeffrey Barnard. An elderly man with a beard and pork pie hat was thumping out old standards on the honky tonk piano. It could all be scenes from an Ealing Comedy.

It was warm enough for them to sit on one of the benches outside. Freddie still had a social cigarette, as he called it, although Arwyn had given up long ago.

'I got a message from Bren last night,' he said, pouring out the bottle of red.

'Your brother? Thought you were never in touch.'

'So did I. But it appears he's got cancer.'

'I'm sorry to hear that.'

Freddie was from the branch of the family who'd moved up to London to run a dairy near Paddington years and years ago. Arwyn had taken him to the farm a couple of times when he was a small young boy, and so he knew some of his distant relatives.

'How has that left you feeling?'

'A good question,' said Arwyn with a sidelong glance. 'Perplexed, I suppose, is the word that comes to mind.'

'You'll have to get yourself checked out. What kind of cancer is it?'

'He didn't say.' Freddie always had a knack of homing straight in to the nub of a thing.

'Are you going to see him?'

'I don't know,' said Arwyn, feeling somewhat pathetic. 'It all seems so, well, unreal.'

'You have to. He's reached out to you. You have to go and find some answers.'

Arwyn liked the way he put it - operational, something that just had to done. Arwyn thought he did indeed need answers.

From there they proceeded to Café Bohème, where an excellent jazz duo were playing, and then to Freddie's favourite sushi place on Frith Street, where they sat on cushions with their feet in a well under the table as he ticked off the choices on a long piece of paper.

They said their fond farewells about four. Freddie still liked his hugs. When Arwyn went to his army passing out parade in Winchester, Freddie said in a gruff voice when it was all over, 'Can I 'ave a 'ug?''

'A hug? You're a big grown up soldier now.'

He changed to a high squeaky childish voice: 'But it's still me inside.'

Arwyn had been under strict instructions not to try to hug him in front of his army mates. Freddie had rung him the night before with a list of how he should behave and what he should do.

'And don't say anything about our glamorous lifestyle.'

'What glamorous lifestyle?'

'You know, living in Central London, going out in Soho and the West End. Most of the lads here are from council estates oop North.'

'Remember,' were Freddie's parting words now, 'go to Wales. Klapperslanger.'

Freddie had adopted this as some kind of code word when Arwyn had come back from filming in Berlin and had discovered, for some forgotten reason, that it was German for rattlesnake. Freddie delighted in it and decreed it should be a secret signal between them. Arwyn was never clear about what exactly it was meant to signal - something of importance between them, he supposed. But somehow he would remember it.

Arwyn made a pretence of striding out towards Marylebone Lane, but as soon as he was sure Freddie was out of the way, he hailed a cab. He didn't know why exactly he kept up this charade of being fitter than he was - pride, he supposed. When he was younger Freddie had this kind of fantasy of looking after Arwyn in his dotage. This appeared to consist of pushing him in a wheelchair equipped with an ashtray on one arm and a wine glass holder on the other.

Arwyn didn't particularly mind growing old, but he did resent the aches and pains, the stiffness and breathlessness, the dwindling sense of possibilities. Life used to be endless possibilities, but now it was ending possibilities. He sometimes chewed over the symptoms with some of his old partners in crime at the Headline Club for aged hacks on the Euston Road. They called these sessions Organ Recitals, when they would in turn catalogue their various ailments. One said there were three ways of knowing you're growing older: appointment listening to the Archers, secret relief when social engagements are cancelled, and you can't remember the third. He'd always rather scoffed at the radio soap, with the do-gooder Archers and ne'er-do-well Grundys who bore no relation to the people he'd grown up with. Radio 4 was sometimes on in the background on Sunday mornings, and it was the storyline of Helen's abuse by Rob that gripped him. He thought it was excellently done. Yes, he did feel good when he found out he didn't need to go out for the evening. And his memory was becoming a real problem.

Then there were the accoutrements of old age. The Fflint males kept their hair, thank God, so there was no need for comb-overs. He had developed a penchant for cardigans - they were so handy - but he told himself they were back in fashion. And there was that bowl of boiled sweets by his bedside table; they were a source of comfort when the aches and pains came at night.

He made himself some hot buttered crumpets for tea, as he often did on Sundays now, half wondering how all these signs of ageing came about. When did the infinite become the finite? Was it chemical? Well, certainly hair loss and the stiff waddling when you got out of bed were, but what about the cardigans and boiled sweets? Surely they weren't part of a cosmic plan?

Sometimes, when he felt the world was getting too fast or he was getting too slow, or both, the idle thought came to him that maybe it was part of the Grand Plan - that as you got older you got so disillusioned with the way the world was going that you weren't too sorry to leave it. But then he told himself he did not believe in any Grand Plan. Thank God he was a heathen.

He suddenly remembered some lines of poetry his mother often quoted:

What is life if, full of care,
We have no time to stand and stare?

He googled the lines and found, to his surprise, that they were from a poem called Leisure by a Welsh poet, W H Davies, who was born in the Pill docks area of Newport. He spent much of his life as a tramp but in time mixed with some of the highest profile artists and writers of the day: the Sitwells, Jacob Epstein and his compatriot Augustus John, as well as politicians and aristocrats. He became one of the most popular poets of the day, yet Arwyn had never heard of him.

It intrigued him that his mother should know these lines and that they should mean so much to her. He could never remember her either standing or staring. The poem went on:

No time to stand beneath the boughs
And stare as long as sheep or cows.

It stirred something long stilled within him. Llwyn Onn was certainly not a bookish or arty home in any way. The only book he could remember as a child was the huge old family Bible on top of the dresser. It was only when the twins were about eight or nine their mother bought them a book each for Christmas - The

Bobbsey Twins. She must have come across them in Griffiths the newsagent in Crickhowell and thought they would be a novelty. They were an adventure series about two sets of twins in the same family who lived in America, so seemed exotic. He and Bren became hooked and in time built up a little library of the books. They had introduced him to the world of books and other worlds through books. Then of course when the twins started getting books for their studies the library expanded.

Music played its part too - not in any formal way, but there was a long family tradition for the men to join the male voice choir. in Brecon. Will had, and Bren did after Arwyn had left - he himself had never shown much aptitude or interest. The brothers used to sing arias as they went about their work in the fields. Occasionally, when the Welsh National Opera came to Abergavenny, their mother used to take the twins. Arwyn once asked his father why he didn't come too and his father had said, 'I'm not much of a showman.' His interest lay mainly in the news. Two morning papers were delivered to the farm, one covering the South and one the North. Then there were the local evening and weekly papers. The family gathered round for the news bulletins, first on the radio and then on the television. It gave Arwyn a good grounding of what was going on in the world and how it was reported, he now recollected.

His mother used to take them to plays put on by the amateur society in Crickhowell - mainly standard repertory numbers. *The Ghost Train* was one that particularly stuck in his mind, perhaps because their maths teacher played the Arthur Askey part.

Now he came to think of it, there was at least one other book in the farmhouse. It was called Hucklebones, about a horse who could not go to the village dance because he did not know how. The rabbits of the wood taught him by weaving themselves around his legs so he'd pick them up in rhythm. His grandmother had taught him to read it. She'd walk over from her farm in the afternoon and trace the letters with her finger until he'd gone through it. He couldn't go to school until he'd done it. It seemed perfectly normal at the time, but it was only later that this struck him and his brothers as strange. Why did this uneducated farm-woman insist that her grandsons couldn't go to school until they could read? What it meant was that they were always advanced for their age. He and Bren went to nursery school at the age of three, and while other children clung tearily to their mothers on that first day, the twins had spotted a climbing frame - a kind of rope net tented over a crossbar - and ran to it without giving Nell a second glance. Or so she told them later in life. She would add that she was glad to get them off her hands, so naughty as they were. Double trouble, she used to call them. Or twice as nice, on the rare occasions they did something to please her.

He still had that book on his shelves somewhere. It took him some time to find it but when he did he pounced on it like treasure trove, and leafed through it, his hands trembling slightly.

He thought of Freddie's words. Yes, he knew deep down somewhere he should go. The doctor could wait. He rifled through the bulging filofaxes in his desk drawer until he came across his personal address book. He flicked the dog-eared pages until he found the entry Llwyn Onn. The number was bound to be the same.

He dialled the number almost gingerly, not knowing what to expect. But it rang and rang and rang out. He put down the receiver slowly, considering what this meant. He knew now he would have to go for sure. He thought for a while. He'd ring Martin, Will's son, who now farmed Llwyn Onn with his own sons. That too would be an awkward call. The phone was picked up quickly. It was Martin.

'Hullo?'

'Hello. It's Arwyn here.'

A short pause.

'Well, well. Hullo.'

'How are you?'

It was odd how one often falls back on the smallest of small talk when big talk is required.

'Oh fine. You?

'Yes, fine. I got a message from Bren saying he was ill. But I just rang Llwyn Onn and there's no answer.'

'No. He was taken to Nevill Hall Hospital this afternoon.'

'Is he going on OK?'

'Well, as well as can be expected in himself, I suppose. But it's not looking good.'

'I was wondering if I should come down.'

'Well, I wouldn't wait too long if I were you.'

Arwyn digested this sobering update. He suddenly had so many questions he wanted to ask his nephew.

There were so many gaps, so much to catch up on. But he realised it was unfair to do it on the phone like that, to put him on the spot like this. The die seemed to be cast.

'I could get the afternoon train tomorrow.'

'I'll pick you up at Abergavenny. We can - er - have a good catch up then.'

Arwyn wondered if he caught something akin to amusement in his voice.

He opened his laptop and after quite a bit of frustration and swearing he managed to book a ticket. He hesitated over the One Way or Return buttons, and before pressing one wondered when Single became the more American One Way. He couldn't really say when he would be back, although he didn't intend to stay more than a few days.

He eased himself into bed with a groan but also a sense of relief that a decision had been made. He popped a boiled sweet in his mouth. No, he didn't really mind getting old and wasn't even unnerved by the thought of death. He'd seen enough of suffering in old age - his mother lived into her nineties - to believe that people were living too long these days, ending up just sitting in the hereafter's waiting room. He didn't understand the modern fad for prolonging life as long as possible. Surely it was about quality, rather than quantity. He recalled an evening's drinking in Abergavenny with his brother Will when both were still smokers. They were discussing the penalties of the habit and Will said, 'Well, you don't want to be sitting in Plas Cae Cwm pissing yourself when you're ninety, do you?'

That was certainly true. Plas Cae Cwm was the local old folks' home. He was not one of those poor people who faced the end with regrets about all the things they'd never achieved. He was lucky in that many of his childhood dreams had been fulfilled, and he'd had a most interesting life. He couldn't complain, but the world no longer pleased him. He couldn't help feeling it was becoming a hateful place, what with the rampant materialism and the rise of rightwing populism.

But he didn't want to go yet. No, not just yet.

3.Mondays are royal blue

Arwyn was half way to Paddington when he realised he'd forgotten his earphones. He'd downloaded some dramas from Radio 4 Extra to listen to on the train journey. It was another source of solace in this enfeebled state. He turned to it more and more as, in his opinion, television was being given over to complete trash. The entire nation seemed to be talking about Strictly or Love Island or Game of Thrones, let alone the so-called realities such as Towie or one he saw about people from the Welsh Valleys subtitled The Filthy Bits. He was not easily shocked - he'd seen a lot in his career - but he found this quite disgusting. It was not their language or even their sexploits, more the fact that they cheerfully told the world about them. He considered it sheer exploitation of fame-hungry youngsters who had nothing much else to look forward to now all the mines and industry had been shut down.

He knew that he'd had it good in life and should not be sniffy about people who had not. He was not one of those who faced the end regretting all the things that have never been achieved. Many of his dreams had come true in one way or another and no-one could say his life had not been interesting. He did feel privileged when he looked back on it. So he thought that when the end came he would be ready for it.

He ducked into an electronics shop to get more earphones, thinking as he did so that he was making a mistake. He knew they would be expensive, but ordinary ones wouldn't do. His blasted new phone needed one with a jack instead of the commonplace pin: all a ploy to get you to spend more money, of course.

These places always unnerved him now. They seemed to be full of school-age assistants who stood around being unhelpful and not knowing anything when you did eventually manage to engage their attention. He approached an exceptionally young man who look startled to be asked a question. He was directed right to the back of the huge floor, to the shelves on the left. When did sales assistants stop going to get things for you? It took him quite a while to look through the myriads of accessories only to find that what he wanted was not there. He waylaid another salesman, and told him exactly what he needed. He was led all the way over to the shelves on the right. A thorough search of the wares on display revealed the item was not there either. Without a word, the guy disappeared through a door at the back, and Arwyn could only assume he'd gone to check in the store- room. He came back with a small white box whose label said £27. Arwyn handed over his card and when it went through said he was going to check it was the right one as he'd been caught out like this before. He opened it with some difficulty, while the guy looked on as if this were an outrageous thing to do. It was the wrong one.

'As I said, I need the sort with a jack.'

Wordlessly, the guy sauntered back towards the door and after another long wait came back with an identi-

cal box with a £29 label. It was at least what he needed.

'Can I give you two quid and take this one?'

The guy looked horrified, said he'd have to get a refund for the first one and waved him vaguely in the
direction of the pay desk at the front. Arwyn was
keeping an eye on the time and it was getting rather
tight if he was to make his train. And all this walking
was beginning to tire him out.

He approached one of the tills at the pay desk. After
one or two minutes the woman looked up and said,
'I'm not on tills.'

He queued up at the next one. When he got to the
front and explained what he wanted, he was directed
to the queue at the refund desk alongside. When it was
his turn he wearily repeated his request. The guy
searched in a drawer and produced a sheaf of forms.

'Look, I'm in a great hurry. I've got a train to catch.
For my mother's funeral.'

The guy looked up at Arwyn's white hair and wrin-
kled face, and was clearly wondering how old his
mother would have been.

'I'm afraid there's a process for this.'

'There's one for burying your mother too.'

'I lost my mother too, so I know what it's like.'

'Not if you missed your train and couldn't get there,' said Arwyn.

He knew that his behaviour was really out of order but felt he'd been driven to it and his anger at that moment masked his sense of shame. He'd had enough and calculated that if he was there any longer he might well miss his train. He threw two pounds and the wrong earphones down on the desk, stuffed the right ones in his pocket, said 'I'm going now,' and walked out of the shop.

Making his way as briskly as he could towards Paddington, shame about the lie started to replace his anger. He was well aware that he was becoming a fully paid-up Grumpy Old Man, and was falling into the trap of complaining that things weren't what they used to be. Sometimes he could see himself as if being filmed, but despite resolutions to be nicer to people, he couldn't seem to help it. If the world was now a global village, then it was a fiefdom being ruled over by remote tech Barons and overrun by yobs.

Human knowledge and reason, he'd come to believe, were draining away and being replaced by systems. No-one knew anything anymore. So no-one could make decisions or take initiative without being told by a computer. And don't get him started on call waiting. The other day it took him an hour and twenty minutes to get through to his bank. Instead of 'we're experiencing an extremely high volume of calls,' they should blame an extremely low volume of staff so they could make a high volume of profit. And even when he got through to the bank they couldn't answer his question. Why was the simplest thing so complicated these days? Or was he just getting old? Maybe it was a bit of both: not a good combination. In any case, he knew that one of his many failings now was impatience. But when time is running out, the smallest hitch or glitch can seem to turn into a crisis. On the other hand, there was an upside to being a GOM, when you can be completely yourself and complain to your heart's content without worrying about what people think. Coming from where he did, he had for a long time felt an outsider in the world of journalism and media. Outsider syndrome, he supposed it was called these days, now that everything needs a name.

He made the train in the nick of time and slumped into his seat, exhausted. It was a joy to get out of London, especially on this glorious autumn day. The trees and hedgerows of bronzes and golds seemed endowed with a bygone stillness, even as they sped by. Perhaps this was another sign of the waning lifespan, when the long ago seemed so idyllic compared to the here and now. His mother used to recall the summers of her childhood: 'You could hang your coat up in May and not get it out again until September - apart from the odd thunderstorm.' The twins would laugh at her light dismissal of the storms. He fell asleep, with a snug, warm feeling and the earphones remained in his pocket.

He roused as they approached Newport, where he had to change trains. The sinking sun caught that tall building just before the Usk with a strange light that shone right through it and gave it a skeletal aspect. It was as if the real was becoming ethereal, as if little lives on earth did not matter much in the grand scheme of things. It was strange being back in the town where he and Bren took their first tentative steps into nightlife in their late teens and as he got nearer to his destination it suddenly hit him how nervous he was feeling. How could he and Bren bridge the gap of thirty years? What would they find to say to each other, especially in the circumstances? And there was the rest of the family to be faced. What explanations would be required?

He had half an hour's wait. He wandered down Cambrian Road and through an arcade into the High Street. It was even grimmer than he expected and seemed to consist entirely of charity shops and hair extension salons among the boarded up ones. The pubs were bustling even at this time of the afternoon, the people of all ages huddled in the smoking areas outside looking distinctly down at heel and miserable. The young women were what his mother would have described as scantily-clad, which would be under-standable in the heat of summer but Arwyn recalled now that it was a characteristic of the town even in the midst of winter, as young women came down from the Valleys for a night out. The shorter the skirt and skimpier the top, the more sophisticated they seemed to feel. Now, it didn't look a happy city. It was all a far cry from the bustling docks town he knew in his youth.

He found his feet taking him towards Market Street. It was there that the twins sometimes went looking for adventure and girls when they were about seventeen. Arwyn used to feel it was always he who made the running, getting a lift with Will down to Abergavenny and then the train to Newport. Bren would follow on behind, jumping in the back of the Land Rover at the last minute. Arwyn would try to shake him off, thinking perhaps that he would cramp his style. He used to meet friends in the Black Swan, which they knew as the Mucky Duck, before going on to a nightclub. He was curious to see if it was still there.

It was, but in unrecognisable form. The facade was clad in rough wooden planks, with Wild West saloon-style swing doors in front of the main door. It was shut. The memories that came swirling back were strong but at the same time intangible, as if he were reaching out to touch something solid that was just beyond his grasp. It was a dispiriting experience, the here and now mixing with the there and then, and he made his way back to the station with a heavier heart. The flashbacks to his youth just served to remind him how far away it was. A Greek friend had once told him that nostalgia is made up of 'return' (nostos) and 'suffering' (algos).

The Abergavenny train slowed into Cwmbran. It was here that the twins competed in the county youth athletics finals. They were well ahead of their field in the two hundred metres, and the competition was between the two of them. To begin with, Arwyn would usually win. Bren had a flying start and would be ahead at the bend, but this was Arwyn's forte and he seemed to find an extra zip as he rounded it. He would gradually gain on his brother and pip him at the post. As they got older though, Bren became fitter as he was doing more work on the farm, whereas Arwyn took more and more to his books as he geared up for university. In their last race, Bren beat him by a full second. It was devastating at the time, but seemed so unimportant, amusing even, now.

Outside Abergavenny station, Arwyn looked around for Martin and wondered if he'd recognise him. They had kept in loose touch over the years - Christmas cards and so on, and Martin had brought his young boys up for a visit to London shortly after the birthday party and stayed in the flat. He'd shown them around all the sites, bonded with Martin, as they'd say now, and he remembered the younger boy crying when they had to get on the train home at Paddington.

A man in his early fifties jumped out of a Land Rover and walked up to him.

'Hullo, Uncle,' he said, holding out his hand.

Arwyn almost looked around to see who he was talking to, so unused was he to being addressed with the word. But yes, he knew it was his nephew straightaway. He hadn't changed much: greyer at the temples but still that thick dark thatch topping the stocky, muscular body. The face was pleasant - healthy and open.

He grabbed Arwyn's backpack, despite his protests: in his career he'd got used to travelling light with just the bare essentials. You could always wash socks, pants and T shirts. He scoffed at tourists on the tube with suitcases the size of wardrobes. Why make life difficult for yourself?

Martin and he fell into easy conversation in the Land Rover.

'We used to love watching your programme. Anywhere in the world you haven't been?'

'New Zealand,' said Arwyn. 'Never got round to New Zealand for some reason.'

He'd learnt long ago not to talk too much about his travels when he got back to Wales. People sensed it was swagger. It was better to answer questions, if asked.

'They say it's a lot like Wales.'

'Maybe that's why I'm drawn to it,' said Arwyn and he noticed Martin gave a quick, quizzical look. It was only then that it dawned on him that, as he hadn't been near the place for almost thirty years, this would have sounded odd. He'd have to be more careful about what he said.

He was relieved that Martin did not quiz him about his uncles' estrangement, as he wouldn't really know what to say. No doubt it would come out in time.

He'd assumed they'd go straight to Nevill Hall, but Martin sped past it.

'Aren't we going to see him now?'

'He's not in a good way. He was rushed in last night. Seems he'd taken too many pills. I spoke to them this morning. They're thinking of transferring him to a hospice in Newport. We can check tomorrow.'

'You mean he tried to take his own life?'

'It's not clear. We were expecting him down for supper at ours but he didn't come and wasn't answering his phone. So I went there and found him lying in bed, not making much sense. Maybe he was just confused about what he'd already taken. I called the ambulance and they came and fetched him to Nevill Hall.'

Arwyn let this sink in.

'A hospice. So he won't be coming home again?'

'Doesn't look like it, no.'

'Does he have a mobile phone?'

'Aye, but he never uses it. Don't think he knows how. He's not on the internet either, so no email or anything. Had it for a while but something went wrong and he couldn't be bothered to get it fixed.'

They drove on for a while in silence. Arwyn stared out of the window at old, familiar places, which now seemed forlorn and bleak. As they drove through Crickhowell, the people looked as if they were on the way to a funeral.

Martin took up his theme again.

'Hasn't got a bank card either. Least, he's got one but he hasn't activated it.'

'How does he manage for money?'

'Writes cheques. He goes into Lloyd's and gets cash. Or I get some for him.'

In some kind of way, Arwyn suddenly envied his twin, free from the strains of contemporary life, and imagined him quite content in his bucolic haven. Martin broke his thoughts.

'Are you coming to stay with us, or do you want to go up to Llwyn Onn?'

Arwyn hadn't given this any consideration.

'Oh, well, Llwyn Onn, I suppose.'

'Why don't you come up to ours for supper?'

'It's very nice of you Martin, but I'm a bit tired after the journey, and not all that hungry. I can come another night. Will there be bread and milk and things there?'

'Aye. I've been popping in quite regularly to make sure he had enough in. Since he had the diagnosis I've been trying to persuade him to come and stay with us but he wouldn't hear of it. You know what he's like.'

Again, that faint look of amusement passed over his nephew's face.

Martin was a good driver but fast, as many farmers are, and they soon reached the tiny village of Cwmbach, which seemed not to have changed an inch. Time, in the time-honoured phrase, had stood still. It was little more than a clutch of cottages, the village shop and post office, the chapel which seemed no longer to be a chapel, and just above it the family local, The Dragon, scene of many family dos. They passed it and started climbing the hill through the woods to the farm. The way was even longer than Arwyn remembered. As they crested a brow in the road, he expected to see the farm lane to the right, whose verges his father had planted with daffodils which were a real show every spring, but there was another corner, another fork to the right or left until they seemed to come on to it all of a sudden. Martin swung the Land Rover into it at such a lick that they both lurched heavily to the left. Arwyn felt a little dizzy, as if he were rushing back in time.

The rough, rutted lane was the same, but there were no daffodils of course at this time of the year. Much to his annoyance, *The Green, Green Grass of Home* kept playing in his head and he couldn't get rid of it. He'd always considered it sentimental slop. And then, as they started down towards the farm, he caught his first sight of the old family home. The blood rushed to his head. He'd thought he'd never see it again. He sensed Martin glance over at him to see his reaction.

The whitewashed house was exactly as he pictured it, nestling in a hollow and surrounded on three sides by woods. He realised he'd been unprepared for how he'd feel about seeing it again. He'd imagined it would look different, but it didn't. He was pleased to note that the farm buildings had been kept in the impeccable order his father had always insisted on. In

Welsh it would be called ty hir - a long house, with the barn joined on to it.

As he dropped him off, Martin said, 'I'll be up in the morning. I'll call the hospital to see where we're at. And we'll have to decide what to do about Jac.'

'Ah yes,' said Arwyn. 'Jac.'

He unlocked the door with the keys Martin had given him - it was always open in his day - and stepped back in time. The old place looked the same inside too, as the song still spun around: the heavy brown furniture, the somewhat chintzy chairs. There were a few new additions here and there: a larger TV than he remembered, although hardly giant screen, and an old computer on a desk in the corner, covered with a thin film of dust. It was tidy enough.

He dropped his bag, went through to the kitchen and found things to make a cup of coffee. He was glad to see it was still unfitted. He'd become a late convert to upcycling, recycling - any cycling that didn't involve a bike. He was no gym bunny, as he understood the phrase was. Just putting on his socks counted as exercise these days. He sat down at the table and smoothed the familiar oilcloth showing harvesting scenes. He tried to make sense of his feelings which were all of a jumble. Snippets of memories came wafting back like elusive scents, ones that he couldn't quite pin down. Indeed it was the smell of the place that hit him - not an unpleasant one, totally evocative yet somehow indefinable. He remembered that one of Martin's boys when young used to say that anything that came from the house smelled of Nan's sink. He found it all rather cloying and decided he needed some air.

Outside in the yard, he peered into the stables. Martin had told him they let them out to various businesses and the first one was full of dismantled cars and parts. But the smell - the most evocative of senses - was one of horses, the same as when he was a boy. So it engendered not just images of how it was back then, but how it felt in the moment. When the world was young. In the distance, down below, he could hear the mournful coo of wood pigeons and that too reminded him of another time, when they seemed to be beckoning, calling him away.

The farmyard was in good shape. Martin and his boys were obviously good farmers. He did a quick tour of the cowsheds, the barns and the granary, and then decided it was bedtime, even though it was bare-

ly nine. On the way back he pushed open the cellar
door. His father used to winter potatoes there, and
kept apples from the orchard in wooden trays. Most of
them would rot. He would tump carrots - bury them
in the orchard to be dug up as needed. Now the cellar
was empty, apart from a few gardening tools and broken furniture. As he went back to the house, he noticed the little herb garden his mother had made in the
front. She'd used a lot in her cooking - sage and onion
stuffing, parsley sauce, rosemary for lamb. It was still
thriving, so Bren must be tending it. He cast his eyes
towards the corner of the Close, where the twins had
had their Den and which their father had comman-
deered for a hen house. It was just field now, but he
heard the cluck of hens and followed the noise around
the side of the house, where there was a chicken coop
in a fenced off run and three or four hens were scrat-
ting on the earth.

He locked the door of the house behind him and
carefully climbed the stairs, as polished and slippery
as they'd always been. He looked in at his parents' old
room, now obviously Bren's: a radio and a stack of
books on the bedside table. He went over to have a
sprwt, as his mother would have called it - a nose

around. He was surprised to see that one of the books was Chetwin's *On the Black Hill,* a rather maudlin tale, he thought, of twins on a farm in Radnorshire who could barely bear to be parted.

Along the corridor was Will's old room, now obviously Jac's when he came home. There was an old-fashioned cassette player on the chest of drawers and a small TV and DVD player. Then, with some trepidation, he slowly pushed open the door of what used to be his and Bren's room until Will moved out. The twin beds were still there: a poster of Man United above one, and of Chelsea above the other. He found it touching that Bren had kept the room as it was. He sat down on his, and slowly unpacked his few things. He looked at his phone. No signal.

It suddenly struck him as desperately sad that Bren might never see this again, and here he was. He'd always imagined his closing days on a terrace in Italy or somewhere overlooking the sea, sipping a glass of wine. Now, he felt oddly at peace and, climbing into bed, failed to stifle a sob.

4.Tuesdays are primrose yellow

Martin jumped out of the Land Rover early the next morning and walked into the kitchen with that slightly rolling gait so familiar in farmers. Arwyn was buttering his toast - with real butter, now that butter was back on the good for you list. It was local, and reminded him of the butter his grandmother used to make. She used to bake their bread too. Now it was a real treat, but when they were kids they used to prefer what they called milk bar bread - white-sliced with margarine that they only ever had in the Milk Bar in Abergavenny. Arwyn had had some porridge too, and he'd taken to having it again for breakfast after many years of eating on the hop - a lot of junk and fast food. In recent years, he'd taken pleasure in a more healthy diet. He wondered whether this was another time-clock thing, that you turn back to the comfort foods of your youth.

'I've rung the hospice,' said Martin, helping himself to a mug of coffee and sitting down at the kitchen table opposite his uncle. 'Seems he's picked up a bit.'

'They say he's doing reasonably well. Had quite a comfortable night and we might be able to go to see him tonight.'

'I forgot to ask to you - what kind of cancer is it?'

'Well, that's the thing. It's not a mystery exactly, but they can't quite pin it down. Kind of generalised.'

'And what's the prognosis?'

'They're not really saying. But, you know, he's in a hospice. They're not usually there all that long.'

Arwyn took this in. He appreciated his nephew's forthrightness.

'So tell me about it. When was he first diagnosed?'

'Well, you know him.' Again, that glimmer of amusement twinkled in Martin's eyes. 'He wouldn't go to the doctor's for ages.'

Arwyn could well believe it. The family's aversion to doctors was ingrained, from the time before the NHS when they had to be paid. Their brother Will had the tip of his little finger cut off when he was adjusting the plough. No visit to the doctor. It was simply bandaged up and he carried on. Arwyn himself complained of stomach pain after the twins' ninth birthday party. His father said it was from eating too much cake. The next day the pain had got worse. He told his father he was in agony. To this day Arwyn remembered his words: 'Don't be foolish, boy, if thee was in agony, thee'd be rolling on the floor.' A couple of hours later, he was indeed lying on the floor clutching his side, and his father conceded that they should take him to the doctor in Crickhowell. The doctor diagnosed appendicitis and told his mother that half an hour later Arwyn would have been dead. He was rushed to Nevill Hall. When he came home nine days later, Bren had asked their mother if he could still snuggle up to him in bed. These memories now came back to Arwyn in a rush. Martin was continuing his account.

'Bren complained of being under the weather now and again, pains in his stomach, lost a bit of weight and as time went on he seemed to lose interest in life as well. Eventually I dragged him to the doctor's myself. Then there were tests and waits and tests and waits and then they said the C word.'

'How did he take it?'

'On the chin, I think. Didn't say much, although we tried to get him to open up a bit, see if we could help and get him a bit of support, like. Seemed his usual self.'

'And did they give him any indication of…..how long, then?'

'They were a bit vague about it. At his age, you know. P'raps there's not much point in talking about timelines. And everyone's different. He'd had a healthy outdoors life, plenty of exercise, fresh food. None of this processed muck. That can make a difference.'

'And what happened on Sunday?' asked Arwyn. By this time he was feeling very much the outsider, that it was his nephew who'd been with his brother and cared for him all these years.

'When I went up to Llwyn Onn he was in bed, looking right poorly. I asked him what was wrong. His voice was small and he seemed kind of out of it, but the gist of it was that he was feeling very bad and odd, and he pointed to some pills on his bedside cabinet.

'It can take quite a while for people to find the place, as you know, and by the time the ambulance came he was more or less unconscious. They told me to bring all his pills and took him to Nevill Hall. The doctor came and after a bit of shilly-shallying they decided he'd taken too many pills. They tried to get it out of him whether he'd done it on purpose but he still wasn't making much sense. He could of just got confused, or been in so much pain he took more than he should of. P'raps we'll find out more tonight.'

'They seemed to shift him pretty quickly down to Newport.'

'Well, aye, but I suppose there's all this pressure on hospital beds these days. If it's just a matter of making him comfortable....'

Arwyn admired the matter-of fact way Martin delivered this information, and how he summed up the situation. He could only sit there, nodding slowly.

'And then there's this business of Jac,' he said, again aware that all he could do was poke his nose in where others had helped. 'Has Bren said anything to him at all?'

'Well, he just kept putting things off. He mentioned it a couple of times - when he should tell him, what he should tell him - but did nothing about it. Took the usual Sunday night phone calls, but as far as we know nothing was ever said. We encouraged him to make some kind of decision about him, but he never did.'

'What do you think now?'

'I think we need to tell him. Just imagine if the worst happened and Jac was out of the picture.'

'Yes,' said Arwyn with some hesitation, bracing himself for what must be faced.

'Tell you what, we could go down and pick him up in Llandeilo this afternoon. It's only an hour and a half. We'll take the car - much quicker than the Land Rover. We can discuss it with Grace, his key worker. She's nice. She'll know what to do for the best.' Arwyn could see that this was the right thing to do. 'And on the way, we can pop in and see Mam in Plas Cae Cwm.'

Of course. Kitty. She was still alive. She must be well into her nineties.

'Yes, alright.'

'The boys have got everything in hand. We've finished the harvest and it's quite a quiet time of the year. You ready?'

'Just about. I'll swill these things through in the sink.'

'You don't want a shower or anything?'

'Already had one. I am used to looking after myself, you know.'

Martin smiled.

On the way down to fetch the car, Arwyn thought about Kitty. Both he and Bren had been a little in love with her when they were growing up, and naturally competed fiercely for her attention and affection. He could see now that she must have found this quite amusing with her rather brassy sense of humour. He remembered one night when they'd have been nine or ten they slept one each side her for some forgotten reason. It was blissful.

She must have been in her early twenties then, and she was a real glamour puss. She'd always reminded Arwyn of a Hollywood star, something in the Rita Hayworth line. He still had an old photo of her somewhere, feeding a lamb from a bottle. Her hair was done up in what he believed were known as Victory

Rolls: curly at the brow and sweeping down to a wave above the shoulders - the iconic style of the war years. Even in a field she managed to look as if it were a film studio publicity shot.

She came to Llwyn Onn during the War, after she was evacuated from Ynysybwl where her father was a miner. She married their brother Will and never went back. She loved the animals and mucked in with the men. She was a daredevil with a ferocious temper but it was over in a flash. His father told him about the time he went down the yard and found her feeding a young calf from a bottle.

'Kitty, I've told thee before, that calf should have been weaned by now. He's going to be no good to anybody if thee keep on like that.'

Kitty had picked up a bucket of supping, as young animals' meal was called, and chucked it all over him. The next minute she was running down the yard hooting with laughter.

She was a dab hand at the piano. She used to send the twins down to Abergavenny on their bikes for sheet music of the hits of the day. There'd be an argument about who should take it back to her, and one was once ripped in half in the process. She had a good laugh over that. Whoever had the music, they'd race back to the farm to get to her first and tell her what they'd got. She'd have the tune off in no time, and got the boys to sing. One of their favourites was *Mares Eat Oats and Does Eat Oats and Little Lambs Eat Ivy*, although at the time he thought the words were *Maisie Dotes and Dozy Dotes and Little Lamsy Tivy*, as he now assumed was the point. Every time he heard the song, in some old war documentary, he thought of Kitty, longingly.

All this played in Arwyn's mind like an old home movie as they sped down to The Gro, Martin's house on the banks of the Bechan the other side of the valley. In Arwyn's day it was an old woodsman's cottage, but as they screeched to a halt on the gravel to the side of it he could see that it had had a lot done to it, a large extension at the back built in the same local stone. An old outhouse at the back of the yard looked as if it had been done up into some kind of small cottage.

Sioned came outside to greet them. She was very young when Arwyn last saw her, at the engagement party with Martin. He had taken to her then - she was spirited and amusing with a certain wry smile that could have been described as winning. He had not come to their wedding, or for the christenings of their children. Now she was a handsome woman with that same wry smile. She had a certain elegance about her with attractive hennaed hair and he could feel himself beaming at her somewhat nervously. He could understand if she harboured certain resentments against him, and was at a loss as to how to proceed.

'Arwyn,' she said, 'It's been a long time.'

'Yes, indeed,' was all he managed.

They both hesitated for an instant, unsure what the appropriate greeting was, but then she leaned forward and pecked his cheek and each gave a little embarrassed laugh.

Martin outlined their plan.

'Come inside,' she said. 'I'll fix you some sandwiches and a thermos of coffee.'

Arwyn was finding these reunions something of a challenge, but he saw he had no choice.

In the kitchen, as Sioned sawed a loaf and Martin went upstairs to get changed, she said: 'I've been telling Martin to get you to come down and stay here. It can't be very cosy up there. Why don't you? Ham, lettuce and tomato do you? Mustard?'

Arwyn was confused about which question to answer first.

'That sounds lovely. Yes, mustard please. Well, I don't know. I was a bit tired after the journey yesterday. I suppose I just wanted to see the old place, and be alone with my thoughts.'

'Yes, I can see that.'

'It's one day at a time, I suppose. It's very kind of you to offer.'

'Well, you know you're more than welcome here any time, and for as long as you want.'

He was touched that both of them were being so welcoming, without a word of recrimination, a flicker of rancour. And he had to admit to himself that both Martin and Sioned were showing him a kindness that he had perhaps not deserved, were behaving with more generosity of spirit than he had done towards his family over the years.

Sioned wrapped the sandwiches in greaseproof paper and put them in a basket with the flask of coffee. She took it to the car, talking to Arwyn about Bren, and waved them off.

As Martin drove rather scarily towards Brecon, Arwyn asked his nephew how Kitty was doing.

'Bright as a button a lot of the time, and in her usual feisty fettle. They told me she heckles the Chaplain if she thinks his sermons are going on too long. They love her there. But then she'll suddenly go off into her own world. Babbles away in Welsh.'

'I never knew she spoke Welsh?'

'Aye, brought up in it.'

'I never heard her utter a word.'

'Well, like you, Dad didn't speak much. It wasn't quite the thing back then, unless you were in a totally Welsh-speaking part. I dunno, p'raps it goes back to when they used to punish you for speaking it at school. All turned around now, of course.'

Arwyn asked about his sons, Gareth and Aled.

'Well, they went to Welsh high school in Brecon.'

'Are they fluent?'

'More or less. Speak it sometimes with Sioned. I still haven't got much, so they don't bother with me.'

He put his foot on the pedal and they overtook a car rather near a corner. They got back in their lane just in the nick of time before an oncoming lorry rounded it. Arwyn winced and stamped his right foot on the ground. Martin chatted on, oblivious.

'And another thing that might surprise you about Mam. Guess where she was born?'

'Ynysybwl, wasn't it?'

'America.'

'What?'

'Her parents moved over to Pennsylvania in the twenties. Her father had heard that conditions and pay were much better in the mines there.'

'Kitty's American?'

'She was born there, but her mam and dad didn't take to it, so they came back when she was two or three.'

'That must have been quite a rigmarole. I've always wondered about the name Kitty. Where did that come from?'

'She was born Elisabeth and her parents called her Betty. I think when she was little she couldn't say Betty properly and it became Kitty.'

Just before they came to Brecon, Martin took a swing up a steep side road. Arwyn said this was not the way to Plas Cae Cwm, not the old house and jumble of add-ons he remembered in the town.

'They've built a new one. Knocked the old one down for the bypass.'

The building at the top of the hill was quite a nice one, red brick with large bay windows and the odd small balcony, surrounded by pine trees. It had sweeping views of the town below and the hills beyond. Martin led the way up to the first floor and along the corridor to Kitty's room. It was fairly large with a small separate bathroom opening out of it, all fitted out with handrails. A bubbly middle-aged blonde in a blue overall was making the bed.

'Ooh, hello Martin. She's in the lounge, love.'

They exchanged a few words and the pair made their way to a spacious, bright room at the end of the corridor. Kitty was sitting in one of those high-backed chairs by a window. She caught sight of Martin and beamed.

'Hello Mam. Look who I've brought to see you.'

'Hello, love. And here's Bren. How are you?'

Arwyn didn't correct her, but wondered if this was the right thing to do. He looked at Martin for guidance, but he didn't seem to object. They sat down each side of her. Martin took her hand, and she stroked his face.

They chatted away in the conventional manner for a minute or two, then she looked at Arwyn and asked: 'And how are Mam and Dad?'

Again he glanced at Martin, who he thought gave a slight shake of his head as if to warn him against saying they were both long dead.

'They're fine, Kitty,' he said. She smiled, reassured. Moments later she asked the same thing in Welsh. He gave the same answer. She turned to Martin and asked how her own parents were.

'Fine, Mam, fine,' he said without hesitation.

A duo were ushered in, he with a guitar and she with a cowboy hat, fringed suede outfit and tambourine. They started singing country songs, naturally enough, to an attentive audience. Kitty started moving her arms in the style of a conductor, a placid smile taking hold. When you saw documentaries about entertainment in such places, thought Arwyn, there was something sad about it, melancholic. Perhaps the producers deliberately chose those kind of clips. Not so here: the pair were very good and seemed to spread joy throughout the room. They finished to a round of enthusiastic applause.

Kitty started nodding off, and Martin nodded at Arwyn that it was time to take their leave. They both kissed her on the cheek, and with a backward glance from Arwyn, made their way out.

As they buckled up in the car, he asked his nephew whether it was better to go along with her or be straight with her.

'Not much point in telling her everyone's dead,' he said. 'She'll have forgotten in two minutes anyway. You'd only be depressing her, and normally she's happy enough. In her more lucid moments seems quite with it and up to date.'

Arwyn had thought about her often over the years and it was wonderful seeing her so well and happy at her age, but there was something sad about what she was reduced to.

And she never asked about Arwyn though, thought Arwyn.

5.Jac

There had never been a clear diagnosis for Jac. It was a very long and complicated birth, but it was after he had the mumps at six months that it was noticed he was not developing along standard lines. Years of tests followed. Some experts thought the issue was the mumps injection, others that it was the lack of oxygen to the brain during birth.

He was a happy enough child in a way, particularly when he was doing something with other people. He loved being out on the farm with the animals, especially when the cows came in for milking, followed by the large but placid Hereford bull. Bren would put him to sit on the bull as he waited in the yard, chewing his cud. One evening the bull took it into his head to walk back up to the pasture, with the sheepdog Toss, as was his wont, hanging on to his tail with his teeth and Jac chuckling on top. Bren caught him in the nick of time. All of the other children around, and almost all the adults, would be wary of a goose with goslings, as she would run at anyone who came near with her alarming wingspan flapping as though she were ready for take-off. Jac would run straight at her waving his arms in a similar fashion. The goose would retreat.

But speech was slow in coming and Jac would often scream with frustration, especially if he was shut indoors with only adult conversation for entertainment. As he grew older, his mother Meryl fought tooth and nail to get him the best attention and special schooling. Gradually he became more or less fluent in his own style. Some of his words and sayings were adopted for general use by the family.

For dishwasher he would say wishwasher. As Meryl pointed out, wishwasher was a more descriptive word, and they quite liked the idea of a real wishwasher - a machine that would wash your wishes so that only the best ones would come true. He was acutely aware of when things should be done and would keep an eye on his watch and give reminders at short intervals. If anyone told him to stop moithering, as they often did, he would say, 'I'm just minding you' - another phrase that was adopted by the rest of the family.

He adored his father's twin brother, Arwyn now reflected on the way to meet him for the first time in thirty years. They'd always been great pals and he had not once mistaken one twin for the other, as everyone else did at some time or another - even Nell. It was as if he had a sixth sense, and had an unerring knack of getting to the nub of the problem if someone had a disagreement or a secret. He would persist in his questioning until he was satisfied with the answers. His mother would sometimes say, 'I'm sure he would have gone on to university if.........' But this was only on a rare occasion when she wanted to include him in the family. She was not usually given to such pointless speculation. In later life, Arwyn came to realise how privileged they were to have someone special like Jac in the family, to know what it is to love someone who is different from you.

Arwyn wondered what questions Jac would ask him now, and shuddered.

When Jac left the special school in Pontypool at the the age of sixteen, Meryl went into battle again and decided that there was nowhere she considered right for him in the county. She heard about this community near Llandeilo founded by a Dutch couple where students would live in houses, not dormitories, and have a whole range of weekly activities ranging from care of the elderly to farm work and drama. But this was out of the county and the county was not willing to pay. They hadn't bargained for Meryl. She banged on office doors, sat in waiting rooms until someone was willing to see her, wrote letter after letter. Eventually, funding was found. But her battle was not over. Nell in particular thought it was not right that they should send Jac away from home and made her views quite clear. Meryl was furious with her mother-in-law and stuck to her guns. When they took him there for the first time, Bren and his wife booked into a nearby Bed and Breakfast for a few days to make sure he was OK. They needn't have worried. Jac took to it immediately and made huge progress in the coming months and years. Meryl had been proved right. Nell, at last, kept her counsel but the close relationship the two had once enjoyed was never the same again.

The small complex was not exactly as remembered, but then few places were. He'd dropped in two or three times in the early days. It was a rather attractive trio of connected Victorian houses in an ordinary street, nothing like the soulless care centre that one might imagine. They followed the signs to reception and told the young woman there they had an appointment with Grace. She soon appeared, quite young herself with short, dark hair and that nice cheerful but no-nonsense face that carers often have. She took them through to a sunny lounge, gave them water and looked at them expectantly.

'As I think I told you on the phone, Jac's Dad is in a hospice in Newport,' said Martin. 'It looks as if he can't have long. We don't know what Jac knows, if anything. We've come to take him home.'

Grace nodded calmly.

'That's probably for the best. We do prepare our students in a general way for older loved ones like parents dying. I think it's only right that it comes from you. I'm not passing the buck but in our experience it's what works best.'

'How do you think he'll take it?' asked Arwyn.

Grace swallowed.

'It's hard to tell. As you know he gets quite anxious sometimes about the small things, but often takes the bigger things in his stride. In recent visits home he came back a little stressed and didn't want to say much, but I inferred that he was upset about seeing his Dad getting older, not being able to do the things with him he used to. He probably understands more than we think.'

'Do you tell your…….' said Arwyn, searching for the correct word.

'Students,' said Grace.

'Do you tell your students about what happens to their loved ones when they die?' asked Arwyn, feeling like an interloper but eager to know. It was the journalist kicking in, and he sensed that Martin was not asking questions. Maybe he already knew the answers.

'We're not a religious charity,' said Grace, maintaining her composure, 'so we leave that up to each individual's family. We do talk in general ways about people being in peace after they decease. But we do encourage students to talk about things like this and ask any questions.'

'As far as you know, did Jac ask you or any of your staff questions about his Dad dying.'

'I know that he didn't. As I say, he can take big things in his stride.'

They talked a little more on the best approach to take in telling him. 'Be as direct as you think appropriate, but don't overload him with details, unless he asks,' said Grace. 'Take your lead from him.'

She gave them all the time they needed and when they had no more questions, said she'd go and get him. She'd more or less packed a bag for him so it shouldn't take long.

Arwyn drummed his fingers on the table and took several gulps of water. He was very much reassured by what Grace had said but was nervous about meeting his nephew. Martin gave him a slight frown.

Grace came in carrying a holdall with Jac trailing behind her.

'Hello, Aw-in,' he said, as he always had, then beamed and gave him a hug. It was as if they'd seen each other a few weeks ago. Arwyn would have recognised him anywhere - a little greyer round the back and sides, certainly podgier - but the same frank, boyish look and the gurgling laugh like bathwater going down the plughole. People used to say he had the face of a choirboy, and in some ways he still did.

It was quite a tense journey back; at least it was for Martin and Arwyn as they still hadn't agreed on what and when to tell Jac, who sat in the front and looked as if he were out for a ride in the country. Martin spotted an old wayside inn advertising lunches and suggested they stop for lunch, even though they had Sioned's sandwiches. They could have them later. Arwyn took this as a sign that they should talk about it to Jac in the pub.

They sat in a window with the sun streaming in the leaded panes and had burgers and pints. Jac looked in his element. When they'd finished their food, Martin sighed and launched in to what must be said.

'Jac, I'm sorry, but your Dad isn't very well.'

'Oh,' he said, and thought for a minute. 'What's wrong with him?' He pronounced it 'ong.'

'It's complicated. He's in hospital.'

'Can I see him?'

'Yes, of course. Maybe not tonight, but in a day or two.'

'Oh.'

Jac turned to Arwyn. He didn't seem unduly upset. Perhaps, as Grace had said, he was prepared for this.

'You missing your brother?' It was one of his constant concerns if people he knew were apart - were they missing each other.

'Well, yes, but he's in good hands.' Arwyn sensed this was the start of Jac's Twenty Questions, with a persistence and precision that any leading barrister would have been proud of in cross-examination. It also struck him for the first time that Jac would look on him as a substitute father, and maybe that's why he wasn't taking the news so hard. It gave him quite a jolt.

'You haven't been to see me.'

'Well, no, I'm sorry, but I've been working.'

'Oh, you was working?"

'Yes.'

'You been working all the time?'

'No, I've finished working now.'

'Oh, I see.' There was a slight pause. Oh I see meant, as Arwyn knew only too well, that Jac was gathering his thoughts for even more intense scrutiny. 'When you finish working?'

'Well, quite a while ago.' Arwyn knew there was no point in trying to fob him off.

'Why you didn't come to see me then?'

Arwyn had tried to prepare himself for this question but he still had no ready-made answer, at least not one that would satisfy Jac. He mumbled something about being busy in London and it being a long way.

'Why you didn't come to see your brother?'

'Oh, I don't know, Jac. We sort of drifted apart for a while. He had the farm and I had my job in London.'
'You been missing me?"

'Yes, I've been missing you,' said Arwyn truthfully.

He guessed that Jac would have heard talk over the years, and come to his own conclusions. However the answer seemed to satisfy him, at least for the time being.

They resumed their journey and Jac again looked around as if he were on a Sunday outing. As they climbed up to Cwmbach, Jac asked 'You staying at the farm?'

'Yes,' said Arwyn.

'You can come to stay with us, if you like,' said Martin. Jac didn't reply, which signalled that he had something else in mind.

'Where d'you want to stay, Jac?' asked Arwyn.

'At the farm.'

Arwyn could see Martin smile in the mirror. He himself was happy that Jac wanted to be with him, but began to have a niggling worry that he would be able to look after him properly.

'Well, I suppose we ought to stop to get something for tea. What would you like?'

'We have shepherd's pie tonight.'

They stopped in the small store in the village and Arwyn bought some lamb mince and leeks. The elderly man behind the counter gave him a strange look as he went to pay. He said nothing as he handed over the change, and didn't even nod his thanks. Although he looked vaguely familiar, Arwyn didn't recognise him although it was perfectly conceivable that he was in the shop the last time he was here. He considered whether he should offer an explanation, behave normally, or pass himself off as Bren. He hovered between the last two, nodding and smiling.

The man said eventually, in a none-too-friendly manner, 'How's your brother?'

'He's going on OK. He's in a hospice in Newport.'

'Aye,' said the man, still unsmiling. 'Remember me to him.'

'Yes, of course.'

Arwyn came out of the shop feeling somehow chastised, humiliated, but he put a good face on it as he went back to the car. He asked Martin about the old shopkeeper.

For the first time since Arwyn had arrived, he thought Martin looked a little shifty as he looked at his eyes in the rearview mirror.

'Oh, he's a miserable old git. No-one likes him. Take no notice of him. The only reason he's survived all this time is that it's the only shop and Post Office around. Otherwise people would have to go into Crickhowell.'

It was quite an indictment from Martin, who usually liked to see the good in people. Arwyn wondered if he'd crossed him or the family in some way.

After Martin dropped them off, Jac wanted to go straight up to his room. Arwyn took up his bag. Jac looked around and looked satisfied and pleased. He pulled out a number of DVDs from his bag.

'I've got my films,' he said. Arwyn remembered he would always get engrossed in a movie when young, especially if it had children and animals in it.

'Let's have a look,' said his uncle. He sorted through them, and although there was the odd action block-buster, they were very much in the same genre: family adventures such as *ET* and *Paddington*. Jac held out his hand for them and stacked them neatly on the dresser by the TV.

'You've got some very good ones.'

'Yes, I do.' said Jac. 'Is tea ready soon?'

Arwyn looked at his watch. It was barely five o'clock. But then, of course, the evening meal, indeed all meals, were earlier on the farm than he had become used to. By the time it was on the table, it would be about six. Late.

'I'll get right on to it.'

Arwyn enjoyed cooking and over the years liked to think he'd become quite good. He found it therapeutic, but just lately realised that he needed to concentrate quite hard on the task in hand. He taken to reciting the steps to himself as he went along, even when he wasn't following a recipe but just knocking up an old favourite or making it up as he went along - what he called a fridge supper. He was also becoming forced to acknowledge that his dexterity was not what it was. Things would get knocked off the counter, sauces would slop all over the place, and ingredients would get lost underneath peelings and packaging. So yes, it required a great deal of concentration.

Jac came down to help him. He found potatoes in a basket on the floor of the pantry. Other than that, the help consisted mainly of hovering and watching him closely to see that the right pans and utensils were being used. No, this is the saucepan for potatoes, that's the knife for onions. All this added to Arwyn's lack of co-ordination, but Jac was useful in knowing where everything was, and would find whatever it was and speedily hand it to his uncle. So between them they turned out quite an acceptable Shepherd's Pie, and they found some peas in the freezer - home-grown ones, of course.

'Very good, Arwyn,' said Jac when they'd cleared their plates. 'What's for pudding?'

Arwyn hadn't given it a thought.

'What do you think?'

'Ice cream.'

'Is there some in the freezer?'

'Yes, there is.'

'Can you get it?'

'Yes, I can.'

After they'd done the washing up, Arwyn suddenly saw the evening stretching out before them. Jac was staring at him with an expectant smile on his face.

'What would you like to do now?'

'Go to Upper Bryn.'

It was the next farm just over the brow of the hill. When the twins were growing up they were friendly with the two boys there. They had a secret society - he forgot the name now - and used to leave coded messages for each other written on pieces of bark in barns and hedgerows about where next to meet and on what mission. An arrangement of stones in the shape of a star would mark the place of the message,

They would build dens in the woods, or go fishing, or make hide-outs out of straw bales. The farm was owned by two elderly unmarried sisters, who had worked it all their lives. Damn good workers, the twin's father had always said, and neighbours all around admired their husbandry. The boys' father, Albert Watkins, had been their workman, who lived in. When he got married, his wife came to live with him at the Upper Bryn, as he was tied to his work and they couldn't afford their own place. This led to the somewhat odd situation that the Watkinses lived in the kitchen and the Misses Davies lived in the front rooms of the house, and did their cooking in the old dairy at the side of the house.

As he grew up, Jac continued the custom of climbing the old tractor tracks up the hill to the farm. They always made such a fuss of him there. He showed no fear passing the chained dogs in the yard, snapping and snarling as anyone passed. In time, they got quite used to him, and took no notice.

'Do you often go up there when you're home?'

'Yes.'

'Who's living there now?'

'Geraint and Mary.'

Geraint was the second son - he'd be a few years younger than the twins. Arwyn recalled vaguely that there'd been some falling out between the brothers, and it was Geraint who'd been left the lion's share of the farm. He eventually bought his brother out - or maybe that was the source of the trouble between them in the first place.

'Who farms it now?'

'I dunno.'

Arwyn felt another wave of nerves about going there after all these years, and indeed whether he was up to the climb. This visit was proving stressful in ways he hadn't foreseen. But he couldn't disappoint Jac.

'OK, but we'll have to take it slowly. My legs aren't what they used to be.'

'OK,' said Jac, grinning.

The ground was dry enough, but there were a couple of shaded dips in the track that seemed to be muddy all year round.

'Have you got wellies?'

'Yes, I have.' Jac always put the emphasis on the 'I' in such utterances. 'You can have Dad's.'

Their progress up the lane was quite slow, but the views as they climbed became more and more spectacular over the valleys below. Arwyn made a pretence of stopping to admire them at frequent intervals. Jac showed impatience, striding on a few steps at every turn. It was a good idea to wear the wellies: one patch was really quite boggy, and it was difficult to find dry tufts as stepping stones through it.

They made it up to the top, and stopped to take in the view of the next valley. A swirl of memories came back - sights and sounds and smells - which he would have been hard put to describe in words. It wasn't far now, and all downhill. The square red brick farmhouse looked the same, but just up to the left of the lane was a newish bungalow.

'Who lives there?' Arwyn asked his nephew.

'Tom and Anwen.'

'Is Tom Geraint and Mary's son?"

'Yes.'

'And do they have children?'

'Yes.'

'What do they have?'

Jac thought about it for a moment.

'Two girls and a boy. Come on, Arwyn'

As they made their way up through the farmyard, some furious barking came from an old pig sty, with two black and white heads bobbing up and down., showing snarling muzzles. Arwyn wondered if they were the descendants of the collies of his time. It was still quite alarming, but Jac took no notice of them whatsoever.

They knocked on the side door, as he had always done. It was answered immediately by Mary, alerted by the dogs. At first she peered through a small crack, looking from one to other.

'Well, well, look who it is,' and opened the door fully with a creak, ushering them in.

'It's Arwyn and Jac.' she said to Geraint, who was puffing on his pipe in the armchair in the corner. Arwyn was inordinately pleased that she'd recognised him straight off. But thinking about it, he must be immediately recognisable as a city-dweller: by his clothes, his face unbeaten by the weather, even his haircut.

Mary gushed over them both, asking how they were, getting them to sit, asking what they would like to drink. Out of a sense of politeness more than anything, Arwyn asked if they had a beer and Jac followed suit. Geraint wanted a whisky. Mary bustled around getting glasses and the bottles from the huge kitchen piece, as Arwyn now remembered it was called, against the back wall. The kitchen was almost as it was the last time he was here, which he couldn't pinpoint exactly: the same stone flags and even the huge black range under the mantel piece. But there was a modern cooker and even a microwave. It was clear that the old couple still lived in this room, whatever the arrangements in the rest of the house. It was large enough.

Geraint was not as gushing as his wife - quite the opposite. Arwyn thought he detected a slight grimace of disapproval on his face as he drew on his pipe. 'How's Bren?'

'Yes,' said Mary, 'We were so sorry to hear.'

She glanced at Jac and then her husband, as if she was worried that the question may be out of place.

'I haven't seen him yet. I only got here last night and he was moved to Newport this morning. We're hoping to see him tomorrow, aren't we Jac?'

'Yes.'

Jac took this as a cue to bombard them with questions about their family.

'How's your brother?' he asked Geraint.

'He's OK, I expect.'

He held out his glass to his wife for another whisky.

'Do you see him?'

'Haven't seen him for a while, no.'

'When you going to see him?'

'Oh, I dunno about that.'

'You missing him, are you?'

'OK, that's enough questions now,' said Arwyn. He recalled the day - Jac must have been about ten - when they went to see Sue, the daughter of another neighbour who'd fallen downstairs and broken one arm and the other wrist. She had her arms in plaster, sticking out in front of her like a mummy come to life in an old Hammer Horror. Jac was transfixed, and his questions were quite polite ones at first. How did she eat, dress, sleep and so on. And then came the inevitable question that would have been on everyone's mind, but not their lips: 'How d'you go to the toilet?'

"OK, that's enough questions,' Arwyn had said, then as now.

Sue, though, had found it amusing and went on to describe her lavatorial procedures in some detail. Mary was equally as unperturbed.

'Oh, he's alright,' she said brightly. 'We're used to it, aren't we Jac?'

Geraint grunted.

Arwyn was perplexed by his attitude. On the way up, he'd imagined a trip down memory lane, the two of them talking over old times. They'd been close, the two bands of brothers, always on the look out for adventure and managing to make their own. The Watkins boys and their wives had been at their fiftieth birthday party, and then it had been a time of happy reminiscence. Before that, on visits home, Arwyn had often walked up to Upper Bryn to see them.

Granted, Geraint's grumpiness might well stem from Arwyn's lack of contact with them all for all these years, but this was something more, amounting to downright hostility. He sensed that Mary knew something, had an idea why her husband was behaving as he was, and she was doing her best to smooth things over. Geraint was hardly on high moral ground given his own fraternal strife. Arwyn assumed from Jac's questioning that the older brother, David, must still be alive. He was nearest in age to the twins, and at one time Arwyn's best friend. He would love to have asked after him, but now did not seem to be the moment.

Jac turned his attention to Tom and Anwen, and their children. No, none of them were married. One of the boys was at home and working with his father on the farm, and the other two were away at university.

'Can we go to see them?' asked Jac.

'Oh, they'd love to see you,' said Mary. 'But stay awhile and chat.'

'Thank you,' said Arwyn, 'but we'd better be getting back while it's still light. My legs aren't what they used to be.' He looked at Geraint and got up.

'No,' said Geraint. 'Things aren't what they used to be.'

It was the longest speech he'd made the whole time they were there.

Before they could leave they had to promise Mary that they would come again soon, although for Arwyn it had been an experience he did not wish to repeat any time soon.

'You're welcome here any time,' said Mary, with what he thought was a nervous glance at her husband. He was staring into the grate, sucking on his pipe.

It had been a bitter-sweet visit for Arwyn, happy memories now clouded by Geraint's attitude and indeed the frailty of the boy he had once known so well. This trip home was throwing up challenges he hadn't bargained for. But Jac looked as if he had had a lovely evening. And on the way back down to Llwyn Onn, Arwyn reflected that despite it all he was feeling more relaxed than he had done for a long while. Maybe it was the good country air, a change of routine and a step away from the strains of modern life. Recently a friend had said of his old mother that she had her anxiety dial permanently switched up to maximum. He'd just had a couple of days away from phone and email, but already he was beginning to feel the benefit, and the dial slowly creeping down. It would have been an enjoyable respite, were it not for the worrying attitudes of Geraint and the old man in the shop.

6. Wednesdays are pillar-box red

Jac was sitting at the kitchen table playing his card game when Arwyn came down. He joined him at the table and looked up for a minute or two. Jac turned each card over from the pack and placed them in four or five different piles, with no pattern that Arwyn could discern. Every now and then, Jac would stop and write some numbers in the notebook he had at the side. Arwyn recalled that no-one had ever quite figured out the rules of the game, as the numbers in the book did not correspondent to those on the card or to the number of cards that had been turned over.

The day promised to be an autumn beauty. As Arwyn was shaving he'd looked out of the tiny window in the bathroom, taken in the view, sniffed the air and already there was that faint hum of a crisp autumn day that he now remembered so well. It was turning out to be quite an Indian Summer. Over the course of his career, he'd rarely had an ordinary morning cycle: sometimes early, sometimes late, sometimes in the middle of the night, occasionally no sleep for two or three days at a stretch. Of late though, as happens to the elderly, he woke early. Getting out of bed was quite another thing: it was painful to find his feet, so sometimes he lay in bed for a while, reading or listening to Radio 4 or Radio 4 Extra. This morning he'd fairly bounced out of bed, maybe because he could picture Jac waiting for his breakfast, and indeed he looked up expectantly as his uncle came into the room. Jac was a stickler for mealtime routine.

'What would you like?'

'Toast and cereal please. And coffee.'

'Bread we have, butter we have, coffee and milk we have. Where's the cereal?'

'On the top shelf in the pantry. With the red berries.'

Jac got up and went to fetch the box himself. He circled around Arwyn as he got things ready, helping to find things but also pointing out any infringements of the kitchen protocol.

'This is the jug for milk,' said Jac, producing a green porcelain one from a cupboard below the dresser. Arwyn had been pouring straight from the carton. He noticed that the cereal was slightly out of date, but it smelled OK, and Jac was happy.

Arwyn had for years lost the habit of eating breakfast, but was getting back into it. He made himself some toast as well to be sociable and also because he felt unusually hungry. Must be the country air. Then he had a sudden idea and told Jac that what he fancied was a boiled egg. Jac said that that was what Dad likes (he pronounced it 'yikes') and said he wanted one too.

He followed Arwyn out to the chicken run and found four eggs in the nesting boxes. He made sure there was enough corn in their feeders and scattered some outside.

The two of them ate their runny eggs and toast soldiers in companionable silence and Arwyn sensed Jac watching his every move. When they caught each other's eye, Arwyn would return Jac's smile.

'What we going to do today?' Jac asked when he'd finished.

'Well, we're going to see your Dad tonight.'

'I know.'

'You want to do something today?'

'Yes, *I* do.'

'What?'

'Dunno.' He thought about it for a moment or two, then his face brightened and he said something that sounded like 'army walking.'

'Army walking?' queried Arwyn. Jac repeated the phrase and this time it sounded more like 'armour walking.'

He repeated the words back to him, but Jac looked confused.

'Sorry, Jac, I don't know what you're saying.' Jac looked disappointed. Perhaps Martin would know.

They cleared the table together. Arwyn washed and Jac wiped, putting things away in their rightful place. As they did so, Arwyn ran through the possibilities of how they could spend the day. No doubt Jac was used to daily routines and activities. He'd talked about them on the journey back: Mondays was serving tea in an old folks' home, Wednesdays he helped feed the animals at a petting farm, and so forth.

Jac loved going out for the day. Alwyn remembered when he used to come home and take him for drives - it didn't really matter where. But he suddenly thought of something he and Bren had loved as kids: the Brecon Mountain Railway. It was a nice climb past the Pontsticill Reservoir and would be stunning on a day like this. As far as he could remember, it went from Pant which was a short drive along the Heads of the Valleys road.

Arwyn dried his hands on the tea towel and hung it over the rail of the Aga.

'What about a ride on a mountain railway?' he asked.

Jac seemed unsure.

'On an old steam train. Toot toot!"

Jac's face brightened.

'Yes, alright.'

They both looked out of the window as they heard Martin's Land Rover roar up with a squeal of brakes and scrunch of gravel. There was a loud rap on the door and Martin walked in.

'Hullo, Jac,' he said. 'And how are you today?'

'We're going on a train,' said Jac, who was good at coming straight to the point.

Martin shot an enquiring glance at Arwyn.

'Brecon Mountain Railway,' he said. 'Jac fancied a day out.'

'Good idea,' said Martin with a smile.

'Tell Martin what you said you wanted to do earlier, about the walking,' said Arwyn, and Jac duly obliged.

'Oh, llama walking,' said Martin.

'Yes,' said Jac with an air of victory, and a reproachful glance at Arwyn.

'We took Jac there once, didn't we Jac?' said Martin.

'Yes.'

'What on earth is llama walking?' asked Arwyn.

'Oh, it's quite the thing now. A couple of farms around do it - they keep llamas and people can walk them around the fields.'

'Good way of getting their animals exercised,' said Arwyn.

'Well, farming isn't what it was. People have to di- versify to make money where they can.'

'You mean you have to pay for the privilege?'

'Yes. If people are daft enough to hand over hard-earned cash, why not? There's one not far from the railway. I can look it up for you.'

Jac was beaming. Arwyn thought for a moment or two.

'Well, how about we go on the railway and then go and walk llamas?'

'Yes,' said Jac.

Martin shot a meaningful look with raised eyebrows to Arwyn, who took the hint as he interpreted it.

'Have you had a shower yet, Jac?' he asked.

'No,' said Jac.

'You'd better go and have one now. Need any help?'

'He can see to himself,' said Martin. 'Although he needs a bit of a push to get there. It's not one of your favourite things, is it Jac?'

'No,' said Jac, and trudged upstairs.

'I've spoken to St Winifred's,' said Martin. 'He's doing a bit better. It's OK for tonight, if we don't stay too long.'

'Did you speak to Bren himself?'

'No, he was having a shower or something, but the nurse was very nice.'

'So will he be alright about Jac?'

'I explained the situation. She said she'd talk to Bren about it and ring back if there was any problem.'

'And what about me?'

'What about you?'

'Does he know I'm coming?'

'Yes,' said Martin, a little too emphatically, and Arwyn thought he could discern a slight shiftiness in his look.

'There we are then.'

'Sioned said to come to ours for tea beforehand - no arguments. Half past five.'

'Alright. Thanks.'

Jac and Arwyn boiled eggs and made sandwiches - ham, and cheese and tomato - and set out.

Arwyn found the road easily enough. As they came into the village of Pant, he noticed someone had rather predictably added an S to the name of the road sign. He wondered how much money the council spent cleaning them off, or whether they'd just given up. He was surprised to see that the little car park was already quite full. The station had been restored to its Victorian heyday, with old trunks and suitcases on porters' trolleys in the booking hall, which was lined with large Victorian adverts on tinplate. Arwyn read on the

information panel that it had taken them years to re-
construct and he had to hand it to those volunteers -
they'd done a great job. The next train was due in ten
minutes and when it steamed in he was surprised at
how big it was for a narrow gauge, and even had a
kind of cowcatcher in front like in Westerns. Jac became excited when it blew its whistle.

'Toot toot!' he sang with a giggle, and Arwyn began
to think he'd come to regret ever using the words.

They had a carriage almost to themselves apart from
an American family at the other end. They climbed
even higher and then started skirting Pontsticill
Reservoir. The ride reminded him of the annual outing
to the pantomime in Newport with his mother and
brothers. - probably the last time he'd been on a steam
train. What was so romantic about train travel then -
the noise, the smuts, the smoke? The journey caught
some of that romance now as they clanked up the
mountain - but some of it must be the romance of nostalgia which filtered out the bother. The hills and lake
under the summer blue, and the gentle rocking of the
train, lulled him into a calm that he had rarely known
in years.

Jac was clearly in his element, a wide smile never leaving him. He didn't pay much heed to the spectacular scenery speeding by, but seemed to be waiting for the engine's whistle which he echoed at every turn. He asked when they could eat their sandwiches. When we get to the other end, said Arwyn.

They ate them sitting on a bank above the lake and below the little halt which was the terminus. They had half an hour before the return trip.

'We having a picnic,' said Jac.

'Yup. Do you have them at…..,' Arwyn couldn't recall the name, '….where you live?'

'Yes, sometimes we do.'

'And tonight we're going to have tea with Martin and Sioned.'

Jac look slightly troubled.

'She won't cook them things, will she?'

'What things?'

'Them things I can't say. Like tulips.'

'Cooking things like tulips?' mused Arwyn.

'From a chicken. She gives them to the dogs and makes gravy.'

'Giblets?

'Yes.'

'No, I don't think she'll be cooking giblets. Then after tea we'll go to see your Dad.'

'Okay.'

Arwyn didn't know quite what to make of Jac's apparent disinterest in his father's illness. He had braced himself for forensic questioning but Jac didn't bring the subject up at all and Arwyn remembered Grace's words about letting Jac make the running. Perhaps it was as she had suggested - he had seen Bren growing older, had talked about death with his carers and was prepared in his own way. Maybe he'd been told by someone else that his father would be going to heaven and one day Jac would see him again. Arwyn himself had no religious faith whatsoever and he was glad of it. Much of the conflict he'd seen in his travels stemmed from the belief that those who did not worship your god were enemies, to be smitten. There was something terribly sad, he thought, about seeing people pray for something they badly wanted, although even he had been known to plead with an unspecified deity in desperate moments. Athletes, for example, who kissed their cross before the start of a race. Why would they think their God would hand them victory as opposed to anyone else who offered up a silent prayer? As far as he knew, Bren was the same. When they were young there were occasionally visits to the Wesleyan chapel in Cwmbach, but when their uncle sent their older brother Will home for talking in Sunday School, their father washed his hands of religion and never bothered again.

'Are you looking forward to seeing him?'

'Yes,' but Jac's reply seemed automatic, for form's sake. Arwyn wondered if he should hint now that the end could not be far off, but he thought better of it. Let things take their own course: Jac would ask questions in his own good time.

Arwyn found his way to the place where the llamas were easily enough. As they drove up the lane, it looked an ordinary enough farm, with recently harvested wheat fields and sheep grazing on the pastures. There were five or six gleaming cars parked in the yard - too clean for farmers' cars - and signs saying 'Llamas this way'. They led to the stables, where a small group of families were gathered. Two young women were leading the llamas out and pairing them off with their walkers. Arwyn hoped there'd be one left for Jac when it came his turn. There was, and Arwyn was looking forward to a little rest but Jac insisted that he had a llama too. He was in his element.

'Like Dr Doolittle,' he said, as he reached up to stroke the nonchalant animal's neck. And indeed they did look like the pushmi-pullyus of the film, apart from the lack of one head. Arwyn felt he couldn't refuse to have one. He just hoped it would be a gentle stroll. He was already tired after all this unaccustomed exercise. The animals were much bigger than he imagined but completely docile and obviously well used to the drill. There was a little kiosk in the next stable door where they were selling bags of llama food (just hay and a few rolled oats as far as Arwyn could see) so of course they had to have a bag each.

The group of walkers set off at a comfortingly leisurely pace on a well-beaten track, with one of the young women in front and one at the rear. They walked down the side of a meadow, across another field, through a little copse until they came to a small steam where the animals could drink. They were then invited to give their animals their feed. They went back a slightly different way but the whole walk lasted only an hour. Arwyn was calculating the time they'd have before they went down to The Gro for him to have a nap, and he was mightily relieved when they got back the farm and he could lay his head down for an hour.

Sioned had set out the traditional high tea for them: ham, pickles, salad, cheese, and bread and butter. Jac gave her a huge hug and started bombarding her with questions about their sons. It was good to see him feeling so much at home.

When Arwyn went into the kitchen to help carry out the plates, Sioned asked him: 'How do you find Jac?'

'Perfectly OK really.' Just in time he stopped himself from saying 'his usual self,' as he realised that he was in no position to state what that self was.

'Is he looking forward to seeing his father?'

'Well, that's the thing. It's hard to tell. It's as if he's not all that interested.'

'He's like that sometimes when he's preoccupied with something. Goes in on himself.'

'Hmm. We'll soon see.'

When they'd finished their tea, Sioned asked about their plans after the hospital visit. The three men looked at one another, each reluctant to come up with a suggestion.

'I'm going to a whist drive in Crickhowell, Arwyn,' she said. 'Why don't you come? You used to be a dab hand at cards. Mart can drop you off at the village hall and I can drive you back.'

'Well, I….,' and he glanced furtively at Martin.

'Yes, go on,' said Martin. 'Take your mind off things. Jac and me can watch a film here, can't we Jac?'

'Yes,' said Jac, and he beamed.

Martin drove Arwyn and Jac to the hospice in the Land Rover, the three of them fitting comfortably on the front bench seat.

The hospice was off the Malpas Road as they drove down the hill towards the city. St Winifred's, it was called. As far as Arwyn knew, she was one of the very few Welsh women saints, if not the only one. He didn't know what to expect but as they pulled into the complex he saw it was large, with a school and a church by the looks of things, all fairly new and well kept. The hospice part was at the far side. He approved of its cloistered atmosphere. The last hospital he'd been in in London to see an old pal resembled a shopping mall.

'How are we going to do this?' asked Martin as he whizzed expertly into a parking space.

'Why don't you two go in first and I'll pop in later, said Arwyn. 'We don't want to overcrowd him.

'OK,' said Martin, jumping out. 'Come on, Jac.'

Arwyn had been chewing over how to approach his brother ever since he left London. Should he acknowledge their long years of silence and if so, should he look for answers? Were there any? He had come to no conclusions and sat in the Land Rover pondering these same questions. It felt a lot later than it was - visiting, he knew, finished at 8 o'clock but the nights were drawing in.

They could only have been twenty minutes or so. Martin looked somewhat shaken and Jac was quiet and pale. They got him into the front seat and Martin said quietly, "Nursey says you can only have five or ten minutes. He's very weak.'

Arwyn did not know what a hospice looked like inside - in fact he had sometimes wondered - but it seemed like an ordinary, well-equipped hospital, with nurses in blue walking around pushing stacks of computers and gadgets. One of them at the reception desk directed him to Bren's room - down the corridor on the ground floor, last room on the left.

He felt nervous as he pushed the door open gingerly. A nurse was there, typing something into a keyboard. She looked round and got up.

'I'll leave you visit,' she said with a smile, a kind of smirking smile. 'Not too long though. I'll be back in five or ten minutes.' Arwyn was relieved to be given a time limit.

He looked over at the bed. Bren's cheeks were hollow and his pallor was grey. He looked awful. He was connected to wires and tubes and his mouth was covered with an oxygen mark. He took this off when he saw who was there and said, 'Well, you took your time.'

Arwyn had forgotten Bren's knack for getting straight to the nub of things and summing it up in few words. Handy trick for a journalist too. They must have got it from somewhere. Now that he thought about it, their family had this laconic style but were good story-tellers. Before wireless and TV, he supposed, it would have to do for a winter evening's entertainment. They'd be sitting round the fire: Llwyn Onn was such a cold house before they had central heating put in. You would sit in front of the fire and roast, but your back would still be freezing. There was hard frost on the inside of your bedroom when you woke up. The flannel in the washroom was board-stiff.

'Yes,' he said, pulling up a chair alongside Bren's head. I suppose I did.'

'Recognise the nurse?' asked Bren.

He didn't want to dwell on the immediate past, then. He'd take his cue from him.

'There was something vaguely familiar about her, now you come to mention it.'

'Remember Sally Mumford at school?' Bren's words were slow and halting and somewhat slurred. 'Real live-wire. Shirley's her daughter. Just like her.'

'So how're you feeling?'

'Like death warmed up, if you want the truth.' Bren wasn't one for soft words and a bedside manner.

'Is that the illness, or the drugs, or what?'

'My own fault really. I was feeling crap on Sunday and took an extra dose of the meds. Made me feel far worse and sent me doolally. Made me see that the Swiss Option was not the answer.'

Arwyn knew that by Swiss Option he meant ending it all. Bren would see it out. He could see that talking was a great effort for him, and so he launched into a monologue about his life in London, but then saw that Bren was not really interested. He then thought he'd describe his feelings about coming back to Llwyn Onn, but that would only serve to highlight how long he'd been absent. In the end he recounted the day he'd had with Jac on the railway and with the llamas, and how much he seemed to enjoy it. Even that seemed the wrong thing to say, as if Jac didn't care about his father. Arwyn gradually ground to a halt.

'Don't bring the boy here if he doesn't want to come. He'll tell you. Don't think he likes seeing me like this. And I don't like seeing him upset.'

Shirley came in with that sprightly, no-nonsense way that nurses seem to perfect.

'I have to change his drip,' she said. Arwyn was sitting in front of it. He stood up to get out of the way. 'Here, you can do it for me. Just swap the old bag for this and make sure the goldfish is under the squiggly line.'

Both brothers let out little snorts of laughter.

'Time, gentlemen please,' she said when they'd finished. It had been a sad visit in many ways, with nothing resolved about their estrangement. But at least, maybe, some ice had been cracked, if not broken.

'I'll be in tomorrow night,' Arwyn said to Bren. 'Perhaps you'll be feeling better and we can have more of a chat.'

'Perhaps,' said Bren, and raised his hand slightly in a feeble goodbye.

Shirley walked back with Arwyn to the main entrance.

'Is it going to be like that now - downhill all the way. Or might he be feeling a bit brighter tomorrow?' he asked.

'Quite likely. That overdose knocked him for six, whether it was intentional or not.'

'I don't think he meant it.'

'Is that what he told you?'

'Yes.'

'Do you believe him?'

'Yes, I do.'

'Well, that's something then.'

'But he won't be coming out of here?'

'Probably not.'

'Any idea how long?'

'They can't say. Could be weeks, or months, or.....'

'Days?'

'Aye. Everyone's different. Look, I'll give you my mobile. You can give a ring if you want a chat. Not that I'll be able to tell you much more, probably.'

She took his phone and started pounding in numbers. 'Oops, I'm putting in my hairdressers.' She looked up at him. 'Unless you fancy some highlights or extensions?'

'I'll let you know. Thanks, Shirley.'

7.A murmur of murder

Martin and Arwyn were largely silent on the drive back. There was not much they could say with Jac there, and neither of them felt like small talk. Jac was quiet too.

Sioned was waiting for them in her car outside the

village hall, an old mock Tudor affair with a brick bottom half and a half-timbered effect on the top. Arwyn remembered going to eisteddfods there, singing duets with Bren at Nell's insistence. They weren't very good. He recalled the last time when they would have been about twelve: the set piece was *Lle Bo'r Gwenyn* (Where the Bee Sucks) in two-part harmony which he found a particular challenge. He lost the note in the middle, going two tones higher and continued in the same vein for two or three bars until he got a nudge in the ribs from Bren. They came last, and after that they rebelled and refused to sing again.

He jumped out with something like relief and slapped the windscreen as goodbye to Martin and Jac. Sioned led the way through the heavy wooden doors and inside it had hardly changed at all. The sight of the stage gave Arwyn a slight shiver as he relived for an instant the eisteddfod disgrace, and then he surveyed the two rows of tables stretching the length of the hall. Most seats were already occupied.

'Ah, the youth section,' said Arwyn, and Sioned's sardonic smile reminded him that he was probably one of the oldest there, although not by much. Ladies, as they were called, routinely outnumbered gentlemen, so it was easy for him to find an appropriate place, but Sioned had to play as a gentleman too. They sat next to each other across the table from two ladies: they would partner the ones diagonally opposite for the first hand.

They exchanged brief hellos, then Sioned ran him through the form. If the gentleman won he would move up to the table on the left. If he lost he would move into the other gentleman's chair and play with the other lady. You kept your running score on your card.

He just about remembered it. The Fflints had always been great card players. It was a Boxing Day staple: the table would be cleared after dinner and covered with a green baize cloth and ashtrays, bowls of nuts, and whisky would be put in the corners. From the age of about ten their father allowed the twins to have cider: they used to make it on the farm and he considered it only mildly alcoholic.

Arwyn thought he'd easily be able to keep up with the old dears but he had to think again. They snapped down the cards like regular cardsharps, filled in their scorecards in a flash and moved nimbly to their next position. He and his partner lost, so Sioned moved to the next table and he took her seat, ready for the next lady.

As the evening progressed he got into the swing and rhythm more and was lucky with his cards. He sensed some of them recognised him - whether this was because of the family likeness or word had got around, he could not have said. A few said hello and a couple asked after his brother. But others gave him a frosty look and the curtest of nods. One old man positively recoiled when he said he lived in London. And one or two ignored him altogether. Their conversation was mainly in English but at some tables they spoke in Welsh. Arwyn just about held his own on a basic level.

At the interval for tea and biscuits, Arwyn went to join Sioned at her table, although it seemed to be the done thing to stay where you were.

'How're you doing?' she asked.

'Picking up a bit,' he said. 'But I can't help feeling I'm getting some funny looks.'

For just a moment, she seemed stumped for what to say, which was very unlike her.

'Well, it's natural I suppose, stranger in town and all that.'

'But some of them seem to recognise me.'

Sioned opened her mouth but was cut short by an announcement in Welsh that it was Alf's eightieth birthday and they all sang happy birthday in the language.

Arwyn's luck continued in the second half. Towards the end he found himself sitting next to a guy who'd been studying him quite intensely since he'd caught his eye. Arwyn felt a little nervous. After the hand was played, the guy said to him, 'You don't recognise me, do you?'

Arwyn looked at him more carefully: he was a well-kept man about his own age, and indeed there was something vaguely familiar about him.

'Derek? Derek Parkes?"

Derek smiled briefly.

'I hear Bren's not doing so well.'

'No. He's in a hospice in Newport.'

'Sorry to hear that. Remember me to him.'

The three had been in the same class at Brecon High. Derek had first been Arwyn's best friend, then Bren's. The twins tended not to share friends and as they got older and started striking out for their independence they moved in different circles.

'You still in London?'

'Yeah. You?'

'I was a vet here in Crickhowell all my life. Widower now. A couple of kids living away.'

It was time for him to move for the last hand, so they nodded byes.

When it was over and they totted up the scores, Arwyn had come top of the gentlemen. As he went up to collect his ten pound prize, someone shouted, 'Go back to London!' and there was a ripple of laughter. He couldn't tell if it was a joke or not.

Derek was hovering at the door, as if he was waiting for them.

'Hello, Sioned,' he said with a nod. 'Arwyn, why don't you and I go up to The Dragon for the last hour, catch up on old times?'

'Well.....' Arwyn glanced at Sioned. He quite fancied a couple of pints with his old friend but didn't want to put Sioned out.

'Yes, go on. Do you good. I can come and pick you up later and take you and Jac back.

There were only a couple of old-timers hunched over the bar when they got to the pub in Cwmbach. Arwyn wasn't sure whether he recognised them or not, or whether he should, but he gave them his short nod which by now was well-practised. The Dragon had always been the Fflint's local and again he was relieved to find that it must have changed hands and Val was no longer reigning over her domain. Hardly surprising, when he came to think about it, as she must be into her nineties by now. In her place was a woman in her thirties, Jackie, who didn't look too pleased to see these latecomers - or maybe it was that frosty look meant for him which was becoming all too familiar. He was getting pretty fed up of it.

He felt like a large V&T but followed Derek's lead and made do with a pint of lager as somehow more in-keeping. They settled down in corner seats and seemed to pick up where they had left off, as good old friends often do.

'You could always make me laugh, Derek,' said Arwyn. 'I remember once we were in Miss Davies' class and for some reason we were talking about cruises…'

'And I said I'd been on a cruise.'

'And everyone was amazed, and then you said your family were driving to Devon and you cruised along.' They both chuckled again now.

'You were sharp, though. I think it must have been the same class and Miss Davies was talking about cars with brighter headlights and asked if anyone could see the drawback in that and no-one could.'

'I don't remember that.'

'And then you said brighter lights would mean cars would go faster so there would be more accidents.'

'It was always you and Bren who came top of the class, though. One or the other.'

'Well, I suppose we were always in a race against each other. Have you seen much of him lately?'

'Not lately, no. The odd visit to the farm when I was still in practice. Occasionally bumped into him in Crickhowell. Didn't come here much in recent years. So what's the outlook?'

'Well, it's all a bit uncertain. It's a kind of generalised cancer which I'd never really heard of before. I was chatting to Sally Mumford's daughter who's a nurse at the hospice. Remember Sally?'

'Who could forget her? Still going strong, I believe.'

'She was saying that it could be days or months.'

'Well, Bren's a tough old bugger. You Fflints always were.'

'I dunno. When it's something like that, you wonder if it's worth the fight.'

'Where there's life…..'

'Suppose so.'

Arwyn felt so comfortable chatting away to his old pal that he found himself telling him how difficult it was being back here and meeting what could only be described as hostility. Derek looked uncomfortable for the first time that evening.

'You can understand it in a way,' he said. 'You haven't been back here for years. Word gets around, especially among the farmers. I'm not excusing them for their judging you, but you know what they're like around here.'

'Did Bren ever say anything along those lines?'

'Not that I ever heard, no.'

Derek changed the subject abruptly and started asking Arwyn about his career: places he'd been, people he'd interviewed - the usual catalogue of questions. Arwyn always got rather bored in reeling off his stories to order like this. He liked telling stories but preferred it when they cropped up organically in conversation, as it were. In the days when he used to return home, he had tried to avoid lording it over the locals who, to his mind, had had less interesting and exciting lives than his. He told Derek a couple of anecdotes which usually went down well but was unwilling to let his theme go at that. He was watching his friend carefully.

'There's something else. Something you're not telling me.'

Derek looked anxious.

'Come on, man. If you can tell a farmer his best tup's for it, surely you can give it to me straight.'

Derek took a deep breath and said, 'Well, if you want the truth, there were a couple of malicious tongues who reckoned you... murdered your wife.'

'Good God.' Arwyn took a moment to digest this.

'Which one? I had three you know.'

'Your second one, I think. There was something in the papers about it.'

'But she was killed in a burglary at our flat. I was away filming in the North somewhere.'

'The papers said you were questioned by the police. I'm not saying I believed a word of it, mind. But you wanted to know what certain people were saying.'

'Which certain people?'

'Oh, I couldn't tell you that. Maybe it was only one - that's all it takes. No smoke without fire and all that.'

'But it wasn't Bren.'

'God, no. At least, not that I ever heard.'

'Was he aware of it - the rumour?'

'No idea.'

'Did he ever speak to you about me? Complain that I'd got too big for my boots, never came home?'

'No. I can say that for a certainty.'

Arwyn took a large draught of lager and wiped his lips.

'Of course I was questioned by the police. Husbands always are. The neighbours were questioned. Her family. They questioned the crew I was filming with. They let me go after an hour or two. But they never caught the bastards, so I suppose that opens the door to that kind of thing.'

Derek asked him, with an apologetic smile, if he knew of any enemies who might spread such gossip. Arwyn snorted at the thought.

'There's always someone you cross swords with,' he said. 'I'm sure there must have been some people down on their luck who resented what they saw as a big shot.'

Jackie threw a tea towel over the pumps and called time. They finished their pints and as they got up to leave, Arwyn said, 'But I'll have a think. About the enemy.'

8.Thursdays are grey

Arwyn woke the next morning feeling better, he thought, for the couple of pints with Derek and the vodka he'd had with Martin before Sioned drove him and Jac back to the farm. He'd very much enjoyed their easy chat, despite the worrying revelation about the rumours, and Derek said they should do it again. It had certainly given him pause for thought, and he half-wondered if he should say something to Martin about the gossip, but had decided that he should bring it up with Bren instead, if he was up to it. He went downstairs looking forward to getting fresh eggs and a simple breakfast for Jac and himself, expecting to see his nephew waiting patiently at the table turning over cards.

He wasn't there, and there was no sign of his having been down that morning. Unusual, thought Arwyn, for Jac to sleep in. He was an early riser, and got up as soon as he woke up. He went back upstairs and knocked softly on his bedroom door. There was no answer. He banged more loudly and called out his name a couple of times. There was no sound, so he opened the door and peered in. There was no sign of Jac. The bed was made but this didn't mean anything: he always did it when he got up. He went to the bathroom. The door was pulled to but not shut completely. He wasn't inside, and there were no clues as to whether Jac had been in. He retraced his steps to the bedroom for a closer look. As far as he could tell, Jac's clothes from yesterday were missing, as were his trainers. Maybe he'd gone out for a walk - it was a cold but sunny day - although this would be most unlike him.

Downstairs he looked for the trainers but could not see them, and he thought a coat was missing from the hall stand. He put his own on and went outside, calling Jac's name. He knew he would answer if he heard. He peered into the farmyard buildings with no more luck. By now he was beginning to get just a little concerned, but not unduly so: there would be a simple explanation. Jac was indeed quiet after the hospice visit, but he went to bed happily enough and did not seem overly distressed. But it was hard to tell with him sometimes.

He decided to phone Martin but didn't have a signal, and he didn't know his house number. He walked around the yard looking for one, calling out for Jac at intervals. Eventually he got through and briefed Martin.

'Is there anywhere he might wander off to by himself?'

'He goes up to Upper Bryn by himself sometimes,' said Martin.

'OK, I'll walk up and have a look,' said Arwyn, but as he did so he remembered how much the climb up the hill took it out of him last time, and hesitated.

'Hang on,' said Martin as if he could read his mind, 'I'll come up in the Land Rover. That should get up the lane.'

'Well, I'll start out.'

'No, you wait there. He might come back. I'll only be a couple of minutes.'

Martin was as good as his word and roared into the yard in no time. Arwyn climbed in and they sped off. Even though the ground was still generally quite dry, there was that dip in the lane about half way up under a canopy of trees that seemed permanently wet and muddy. Martin approached it quite carefully then put his foot on the pedal calculating that they could whizz up the other side, but at the bottom of the dip where the ruts were deepest the rear off-side wheel started spinning. He tried reversing but that didn't work either. He knew better than to dig them further in so he switched off the engine.

'Damn. Should have brought the tractor,' said Martin. 'Here, you take over. I'll put some branches and bracken under the wheel then jump in the back to give it some purchase. When I say go, just start off steadily in first and go to the top.'

Martin soon gathered twigs and foliage and packed them in front of the back wheel. He sat heavily on the arch over it.

'Go!'

Arwyn did as instructed. It didn't take immediately and there were a couple of nerve-wracking spins but then it gained traction and they made their way smoothly up the slope. He stopped to let Martin in. He came over to the driver's door and said. 'Shift over.'

'Actually, do you mind if I keep going? I'm quite enjoying myself.'

'Whatever it takes,' said Martin with his mischievous twinkle.

It took Arwyn back to the days of his youth when he loved driving the tractors and Land Rover. Officially, you were allowed to drive a tractor on farmland when you were thirteen, but Martin's father Will used to let them drive sitting on his lap when they were eleven or twelve, and in those days there were no safety cabs. Once he let Arwyn drive a load of hay further down this lane over a particularly tricky set of ruts. The trick was to keep the wheels on the middle tuft and the offside verge so they wouldn't get trapped in the ruts. There was a moment when the front nearside wheel of the tractor started to slip down into the rut and the hay cart behind them started swaying. Will guided Arwyn slowly inch by inch, until they were back on track. Arwyn was proud of himself as the made it down into the farmyard. He thought it very trusting of his older brother - or was it recklessness? Arwyn probably didn't realise - as he now did - how close they'd come to a really nasty accident. Farming can be a dangerous business.

They pulled into the yard at Upper Bryn to the usual barrage of barks. Mary came to the back door wiping her hands in her pinny.

'Well, look what the wind blew in,' she said.

'Hello Mary,' said Martin. 'How are you?'

'Oh, can't complain.'

'You haven't seen Jac anywhere around, have you?'

'No indeed.'

'We can't find him,' said Arwyn. 'He wasn't at the house when I got up.'

'He sometimes goes up to see Tom and Anwen when he's home,' said Mary.

'Oh, thanks. We'll go and have a look.'

They resisted her demands that they come in for a cup of tea and got back in the Land Rover, taking the lane that led further up the hill towards Tom's newish bungalow and then over the top towards the road which ran down the other side of the hill. It was tar-macked so the going was easier.

Anwen had not seen Jac either, but told them that Tom had gone up to the Top Field on the quad bike to feed the cattle. Jac often came up to see them, she said, and liked going out with Tom.

As they got near the top of the hill, Arwyn looked down into the valley below which was still covered in a lingering river mist like a snow-covered lake. It was a captivating, peaceful scene. But his heart was beating fast. In the distance, he caught sight of the quad bike going like the clappers up towards the ridge. It slowed down as it neared a long metal feeder and, as they caught up, they could see the person on the back was Jac, laughing wildly into the wind.

Martin pulled up the Land Rover as Tom and Jac started pouring the bags of meal into the trough and the bullocks rushed towards it. Tom looked up at the pair and gave them a nod and a smile.

'We're feeding the cattle,' Jac informed them, still chuckling.

'We were worried about you,' said Arwyn, and he hadn't felt such relief in a long while. Jac ignored this, and went on with the job in hand.

'We'd better be getting back,' said Martin. Jac stopped pouring and gave a worried glance at Tom.

'It's alright,' said Tom. 'I'll bring him back down at dinner time. You can help me, can't you, Jac?' Jac happily agreed.

On the way back down to Llwyn Onn, Arwyn could tell that Martin was building up to saying something.

'I've been thinking,' he said. 'Perhaps it's better if you two come and stay down with us. Sioned says it would be easier all round, what with hospital visits and shopping and meals and all.'

Arwyn was about to protest: even though he was feeling guilty about what had happened he was enjoying being at the farm with Jac. But Martin ploughed on.

'It can't be easy for Jac being up there without his Dad. Oh, I know he loves seeing you but the truth is that he's found it hard coming back there recently.'

Jac had not come home at Easter, said Martin. They were doing a play or something and he had to stay in Llandeilo. It was clear that he loved it there. When he'd come back for a week that summer, he didn't seem his usual self. Martin found him in the corner of the orchard early one evening crying - something that he hardly ever did. He didn't say anything concrete, but when Martin asked him some questions he inferred that it upset him to see his father growing older, not doing the things he used to do with him.

'It's as if he's readying himself for the day when they'll no longer be at Llwyn Onn,' said Martin, 'and getting used to being over there in Llandeilo more. Perhaps that's what was behind him going out on his own this morning.

'Nothing to do with you of course,' he added quickly, 'just striking out for a bit of independence.'

Arwyn saw he had no choice but to assent, which he did with as much goodwill as he could muster. But Martin's words saddened him. He'd loved being with Jac at the old place, as if he was catching up on some lost time, but now he saw that's just what it was: lost.

'You can bring your things down for tea. And I was thinking that it would be better if you went to see Bren by yourself tonight. Have a good old catch-up and that.'

Again Arwyn made to protest, but again Martin pressed on with his plan. He'd obviously thought the whole thing out.

'It upsets Jac to see his father lying there in bed. It's something he's not used to at all. I'll stay with him. You go.'

Bren had said as much, so again Arwyn gave in gracefully. He and Jac duly packed up their few things and drove down to the Gro at about 4 o'clock. Sioned told Arwyn he could stay in the little cottage - the annex she called it and he wondered who it was converted for - and Jac the spare room upstairs which he was used to, apparently, and thought of as his own.

The annex was upstairs above the garage. It was a bedroom, a little galley kitchen in a sort of alcove, and a shower room. Perfect, thought Arwyn. That's all anybody really needs. It was tastefully done, with exposed beams in the ceiling, stone walls clad with light grey tongue-and-groove on the bottom half, and the shower room lined entirely in slate. Arwyn approved. He unpacked and made himself comfortable. Behind the bed was a shelf of books and he spotted the old family Bible in the corner. He hauled it out, the front cover coming away from the body - the brass clasp that had held it together was broken.

The title page announced it was The Self Interpreting Family Bible. Illustrated. He wondered what on earth that Self Interpreting could mean. He flicked through the next few pages until he came to a page entitled The Family Register - highly decorated panels with names of the family written in copperplate. The first entry must be their great-grandfather, Edward Fflint, born in 1819, married Eliza Griffiths in 1843. Generations followed, then there was a gap of a couple of pages, then he recognised his mother's handwriting, starting with his grandparents, then their own generation and offspring. When it came to his own name, his first wife's name was crossed out, with what seemed a heavier stroke than the rest, before Diana's name was added. Nell didn't approve of divorce. It seemed to him there was some anger in that stroke. At least she didn't live to see Diana's murder, or his third marriage. On the line beneath for Children, there was another stroke, even heavier. But he noticed something extremely odd: their mother had written Bren's birth date exactly one year before the one that was on his own birth certificate.

Shirley was at the nurses' station as Arwyn went in, and when she turned around and saw him gave a broad smile.

'He's much brighter today,' she said, but warned him not to read too much into it. 'It's probably the effects of the pills he took wearing off. Still, it's good to see him more perky.'

Bren was sitting up in bed.

'Ah, there you are.'

'I hear you're feeling better today.'

'Glad I'm not feeling any worse.'

Arwyn had been wondering whether to relate the events of the morning, and decided that it was better to be open, now that the chips were down. Bren said it was probably for the best that they were with Martin and Sioned. But he didn't want to bring up the question of their birth dates. What could Bren know that he didn't?

There was an awkward silence. Arwyn felt that there was so much to say that it was difficult to find a place to start. He tried a couple of conversational gambits, but they didn't go anywhere. There was still a distance between them, and Bren for all his new perkiness was being distinctly cool. Arwyn wanted once and for all to get to the bottom of their separation.

He mentioned he'd seen Derek Parkes the night before, and Bren did now show a spark of interest. Arwyn wondered why. He replayed in his mind the conversation they'd had. Could it be something to do with the murder rumour? Could that be why......?

'How's he doing?'

'OK, I think. But he told me a funny thing.'

Bren waited for him to go on.

'Well, not funny exactly, not at all in fact, but...'

'For Christ's sake, spit it out.'

'He said there was a rumour I killed Diana.'

Bren looked genuinely shocked and annoyed in turn.

'Good God. But she was killed by a burglar.'

'I *know*. I could hardly believe my ears at first. But then some things started slotting into place. Since I got back I've been getting some very odd looks, if not to say downright hostility from certain quarters.'

'Like who?'

'Geraint, Upper Bryn for one.'

'Ah well, he always was a funny bugger.'

'It's been bothering me how something like that would start in the first place,' said Arwyn, giving his brother a hard but surreptitious look. Bren was looking thoughtful.

'Oh, dunna waste too much dundering over that. It doesn't take much. It may have been just that you were in London and had three wives - that's downright peculiar for some people round here for a start. Think I heard something to the effect myself. People thinking EastEnders is real.'

It had been a long time since he'd heard the word dunder, meaning to harp on about something. He didn't know whether it came from the Welsh or was an old dialect word in English. It made him think of a similar word - moithering - which he believed came from the Welsh *mwydro*. To talk crap.

'So you didn't know anything about this murder business?'

'Course not. I'd be the last to hear any tittle-tattle like that. And if I did I'd have '

'What? Got in touch?' finished Arwyn.

So there it was, broached at last. Bren, though, didn't look guilty, or angry, as perhaps Arwyn had expected. More…confused, which in turn puzzled him.

'It's been almost thirty years now since we had any contact,' he said.

'I know.' Bren shifted in the bed, pulling himself up slightly against the pillows and leaning towards his left, away from his twin. Was it a squirm? 'My bum gets a bit sore after a while,' he said, by way of explanation.

'Why is that?' asked Arwyn. 'The silence I mean, not your bum.'

'You tell me. It takes two to tango, you know.'

Arwyn sensed that Bren was holding something back, that he did harbour grievances but wouldn't open up about them. He took a deep breath and launched into his own musings since he received that phone message, that it must have been something to do with their fiftieth birthday party - the last time they'd spoken. Bren knitted his brows, thinking back to the day.

'You know, that business with your ex and the knife and the sobbing.'

'Oh that,' said Bren, and Arwyn knew immediately that there was much more to it than that. 'Yes, Meryl was a bit put out, shall we say.'

'After that, I thought I was a bit of a *persona non grata*,' said Arwyn and then thought he should explain. 'Not welcome any more. So I waited for a move on your part, and none came.'

'I know what persona non thingy means,' said Bren irritably. 'But communication is a two-way street, you know.'

'So you keep saying.' Arwyn felt they were no nearer to an understanding of why they had been apart all this time.

It was at this point that Shirley put her head round the door.

'Last orders, gentlemen please,' she said with a cheeky grin. 'You'll have to call it a night in a few minutes, Arwyn.'

'On first name terms now, are we?' said Bren. His mood was lighter now, as if he was relieved that his visitor was about to depart.

Arwyn stood up and asked Bren if there was anything he wanted.

'You could bring me some reading matter - some papers.'

'Any in particular?'

'As you see fit. The Chronicle's out tomorrow, so I would like a look at that. And some of my CDs. Jac can show you the ones I like. Opera arias and the like. Oh, and there is one more thing you could do for me.'

'Name it.'

'Could you give me a good shave? They don't do it properly here, although they try their best. But I've always had this rough patch just here.' He stroked the area on the left above his Adam's Apple. 'It's difficult to get smooth.'

'I know,' said Arwyn. 'I've got one too, the other side,' and he stroked his. Bren nodded.

Of course. Twins are mirror images of each other. He recalled his second wife - or was it his first? - peering over his shoulder in the bathroom mirror and exclaiming, 'I can see Bren.'

9.Fridays are off-white

Arwyn stopped off at the chemist's in Crickhowell on the way into St Winifred's the following evening. It was much as he remembered it: the satisfying tinkle of the bell as he opened the door, the wooden shelving behind the counter, the pharmacist in his elevated podium at the back. He couldn't shake off the expectation that someone he knew would be behind the counter, and had to remind himself that it was more likely to be their children, or grandchildren, or even - Heaven forfend - their great-grandchildren.

In quieter moments these last couple of days, he had began to worry about his blood pressure pills left on the bathroom floor in London. A month or so ago he'd gone for the results of some blood tests at his GP's. The nurse had taken his blood pressure and couldn't hide her surprise when she saw it so high. He was used to this, and put it down to White Coat Syndrome. However much he tried to relax, it seemed to shoot up whenever he was in medical surroundings. The nurse made him an appointment to see the doctor - a new one, Dr Nguyen, in a couple of hours.

He took to her immediately - such a contrast to the dreaded Dr Davies. She was chatty and sensible and he felt in capable hands. She took his blood pressure three times and on the third reading said, 'Oh dear.' It was 212 over 105. She said, in the same friendly tones, that if it stayed that high he was at risk of stroke or heart attack. He wasn't unduly concerned, although it was higher than it had ever been. She prescribed him some new pills - he was never good at remembering what they were called - ampi something, he thought. Who came up with these ridiculous names? He had a monitor at home and in a couple of days it had returned to normal, although now he was aware that he was doing himself no good.

He explained the situation to the young assistant. She was sorry, she said, but she couldn't do anything without a prescription. Arwyn knew that missing two or three days didn't matter that much, but he would have to think of a way of getting this sorted soon. He set to collecting the wherewithal for Bren's smooth shave: flannel, hand-towel, gel, moisturiser and one of those vibrating razors that he found so effective.

Next stop was the newsagents, where he stocked up with the Guardian, the Mirror, the Abergavenny Chronicle and Private Eye. He wondered if he was overdoing it, and if so, why? That afternoon he and Jac had popped up to Llwyn Onn for the CDs and the player. Jac had immediately homed in on the ones his Dad liked immediately - *Tannhaüser, Norma*, and a couple of aria compilations and one of Mozart. Arwyn was quite pleased with the booty he was taking to his brother.

Bren was still quite perky and more friendly, he thought, than the night before. He splayed the papers on the tray over the bed.

'Hmm,' said his brother, 'I'll certainly be able to catch up on what's going on in the world. That'll really cheer me up.'

'Perhaps it's because of our age,' said Arwyn. 'When we were younger we could always hope that things were getting better, and that we even might be able to make a difference. But now they seem to be going from bad to worse, what with Brexit and Trump and everything. Going backwards, in fact.'

'And so say all of us,' said Bren.

Arwyn was surprised and pleased to hear his brother's words. The Fflints had always leant politically to the Left, born out of a sense of Non-conformism at first, and then, as they gradually lost their religion, a strongly-rooted sense of community and neighbours helping each other. They'd admired Lloyd George, of course, and there used to be a healthy Liberal tradition in their neck of woods. Margaret Thatcher and her Victorian values had changed all that as many farmers embraced her tenet that turning the clock back would solve present-day problems. Arwyn was glad that his brother was not one of them.

'Like most people, I was astounded by the referendum result and I've been trying to understand it ever since,' he said. 'I read a piece about Ebbw Vale in the Guardian by that Cadwalladr....'

'Carole.'

'Yeah. I expect you know her?'

'Yeah.'

Bren gave a nod with an upward roll of the eyes. 'She interviewed this kid and asked him why he voted Brexit. It was like a scene from *Life of Brian*. He asked what Europe had ever done for us. That new college, built with EU money, she said. Apart from that. That new railway station......And so it went on. We were manipulated.'

'Couldn't agree with you more. And I think social media is to blame for these echo chambers,' said Arwyn. 'People only read things they agree with, and they hate and troll and worse anyone who says something different. And they can form an army.'

Bren fanned out the CDs and almost beamed.

'Good old Jac,' he said, "He knows my favourites. Just listening to the *Tannhaüser* overture gives me this deep sense of peace.'

'What on earth's all that paraphernalia you've got there?' said Bren, as his attention shifted to the chemist's bag full of the shaving gear.

'If a thing's worth doing, it's worth doing well......'

'As Grandad The Bryn always used to say.'

'So I thought I'd give you the works: hot flannel, moisturiser, and this little vibrating razor that works really well.'

'Moisturiser? Who d'you think I am, David Beckham? You and your fancy London ways.' But he looked pleased.

Arwyn ran the hot water in the basin in the corner until it was steaming, and soaked the flannel in it. He draped the towel round Bren's neck, put the hot flannel on his stubble, ignored his wince at the heat, and left it there for a full two minutes. He dried him off then smothered him in moisturiser - he'd always found it a very handy substitute for shaving foam when he was travelling. Then he applied the gel, making sure to rub it in thoroughly, and set to with the razor.

'You see, it just scrapes off like crumbs from soft butter.'

Bren made a strange sound which could have meant anything. Arwyn realised he had a captive audience with Bren more or less silenced for the duration, a little like he imagined dentists must feel when they have their patients in their power.

'I've been thinking, you know, about the party and the aftermath and why we lost radio contact. Yes, it was an awkward moment when Annie came in with the knife, but I had no option but to invite her, because her son was doing all the catering. I'd gone to see him at The Dragon to make the final arrangements. Annie was there and kind of assumed she was invited. She just said she was looking forward to seeing us both again. Perhaps I should have explained all this to you and Meryl but, I was busy and travelling and that, and as I said I was waiting for some signal from you.'

All Bren could do was utter the odd 'aaah' which could have meant anything, but Arwyn took it that he accepted all this. So he could strike off the party as a possible cause of the rift. He was more determined than ever to get to the bottom of it. He was nearing the rough patch now, and Bren fell silent. The blades glided through as smoothly as the rest of his chin, and Arwyn felt a great sense of achievement. He finished off the job, wiped the face with another hot flannel, a towel and a flourish.

'There - how's that feel?'

Bren stroked his chin. He looked younger and healthier.

'Very good. Best I've had for ages. Here, cop a feel.'

Arwyn stroked Bren's chin with the back of his hand.

'Yeah, I would say that's done the job.'

'Is that how you always do it?'

'Yes,' said Arwyn. 'Cop a feel,' and Bren returned the favour, stroking the opposite side of his chin where his rough patch would be.

'Hmm. Is this a daily service you're offering?'

'Could be.'

'Same place, same time tomorrow? I'm getting tired now.'

'Want anything else?'

'Not that I can think of. Is Jac OK?'

'Yep. We're doing fine with Martin and Sioned. I'm in that flat they've got above the old garage. Very nice it is too. I was wondering who they did it up for?'

'Well, they've been wanting me to go down there but I couldn't tear myself from the old pace.'

'Unlike some people,' hung in the air.

Arwyn thought about the birth entries in the Bible and wondered again whether or not to bring it up, but decided against it. Bren would be no wiser than he was.

'Anyway,' he said, 'Martin was right. He thought it would be easier all round if we were down there.'

'So did I.'

'Ah. So you were behind it?'

'Don't worry too much about the boy. He knows his own mind.'

'Oh, we know that. It's just that we don't know what to tell him.'

'He probably knows more than you realise. Don't bother about him coming to see me. I know the score.'

'Yeah. We figured that one out too.'

'Ok. Bye.'

'Bye.'

10. Identical strangers

That discrepancy in their birth dates had been nagging somewhere at the back of Arwyn's mind. He'd checked back a couple of times to make sure that his eyes weren't deceiving him. But there it was in black and white - or more precisely copper and cream - in his mother's neat, old-fashioned, slanting hand. He'd racked his brain for some kind of explanation but found none, other than it was a slip of the pen. But it was so unlike Nell, who was so meticulous in matters of this sort. He didn't know who he could ask, just for some kind of peace of mind. There was Kitty of course, but as Martin said, there was no heed on her.

It set him thinking about the nature of twins. Over the years he'd somewhat casually read up on the subject and watched documentaries, although these always spooked him a little. There was one case of two girls, June and Jennifer, in West Wales somewhere which had particularly struck him. They were the only black twins in the region - they'd come with their parents from Barbados as part of the Windrush generation - who were bullied and stopped communicating with other people. They just talked to each other and their younger sister and developed their own kind of lan- guage, known technically as idioglossia - something spoken by very few people. Apparently it was based on Bajan creole. Arwyn identified with this 'twin talk' on a much smaller scale. He and Bren had their own words for some things: o-beeps for windscreen wipers (because of the sound they made) and plastics for car- toons. But this case went far beyond that. They were reckoned to speak in unison and gave an interview for the documentary. Arwyn found this intriguing when he saw the trailer so watched it. But they gave very short answers to predictable questions - he came away thinking that it was no big deal and he and Bren could have managed as much had they put their minds to it.

It was a sad tale. In later life they took to crime - vandalism and theft - and ended up in Broadmoor. While they were there, they began to believe that it was necessary for one of them to die to liberate the other. They made a pact that if one did die, the other would start communicating and lead a normal life. Jennifer died mysteriously when she was 29 years old, and June said, 'I'm free at last. Jennifer has given up her life for me.'

Inevitably the case brought up the question of nature versus nurture - are babies born fully cooked or does character depend on upbringing? Arwyn had always believed it was a mix of both - maybe the balance can vary from person to person, from place to place. In one individual nature can dominate, in another nurture plays more of a role. From time to time when they were younger, friends had suggested to Arwyn and Bren that they take part in one of the nature v nurture experiments, but neither of them was interested. What did interest Arwyn was the concept of the evil twin, which he was unaware of until he worked in the USA for a time. When he looked into it, it seemed to have taken hold with Chaplin's film *The Great Dictator*, where he played both a simple barber and his counterpart, a Hitler-like despot.

His research revealed that this idea is present in ancient cultures. In Mesopotamia there was an epic poem where one twin was 'civilised' and the other was 'wild.' Arwyn couldn't help feeling that there was something in that - Bren as the stolid farmer carrying on generations of farming tradition, and he as the one who struck out on his own looking for adventure. Twin deities often crop up throughout the ancient world, representing the dualistic nature of the universe and the battle of good and evil. There are similar conceptions in many Native American creation myths.

In other beliefs, such as Toaism, the so-called laughing twins represent harmony and joy. For the Yoruba people of Nigeria, they are 'spirit children' who have connections to the supernatural world and can bring good or bad to their families. In West Africa they are always seen as special - as for some reason the birthrate of twins is four times the global average of three per cent.

Freddie, who took an interest in such matters, told Arwyn about a town in Brazil which had the highest incidence of twins in the world. Arwyn got curious. This was another benefit of getting older, he found, that he would want to find things out on the spot - it wasn't idle curiosity. Of course as a journalist he'd always wanted to know how and why things happened, but now, like so many other things, time was of the essence. And if he left it a while he would forget what it was he wanted to look up. Here the internet did have its uses.

The twin town was called Candido Godoi, and the incidence there was ten per cent, twice the rate of the next highest in Nigeria. The notorious Nazi doctor Josef Mengele, who conducted gruesome experiments on twins in Auschwitz, had fled to the region after the war, and this led to speculation that he wanted to carry on his evil work and brought families with twins there for his purpose. Geneticists rejected these rumours, and said the record rate was a result of genetic isolation and inbreeding.

Mengele's twins were initially treated and fed better than other children in the death camp, and witnesses said later he was kind to them. They were examined and measured every week. Then he started infecting one twin with a disease such as typhus and many would die. He would then kill the other twin and dissect both bodies for comparison. Other experiments included amputating the limbs of one twin.

Then there's Castor and Pollux, the stars of the constellation Gemini. In Greek mythology, they shared a bond so strong that when Castor died, Pollux gave up half his immortality to be with this brother in the heavens - half, because they are said to divide their time between the underworld and Mount Olympus, so their constellation can be seen for only half the year.

Back in the real world, another spooky phenomenon that Arwyn came across was that when some twins who had been separated at birth were reunited years later there were remarkable similarities in their lives. James Springer and James Lewis were born in Ohio in 1940. They were adopted by different families and grew up apart and did not meet until 39 years later. They became known as the Jim Twins.

They found that:

* Both were six feet tall and weighed 180 pounds
* Both had married twice. Their first wives were called Linda and their second wives called Betty
* One had a son called James Alan and the other a son called James Allan
* Both had a dog called Toy when they were growing up.
* They were both sheriffs
* Both smoked Salem cigarettes and drank Miller Lite
* Both bit their fingernails.

Now, the height, weight and fingernails struck Arwyn as perhaps only to be expected. And of course, there were many differences in their lives. But all those names? Similar cases were highlighted in the documentary. To believe that it was anything other than coincidence would mean that there was indeed some cosmic force directing their lives. Arwyn believed it was just a remarkable fluke in a strange world where not everything could be explained.

But the most extraordinary case of all he saw was documented in a film called *Three Identical Strangers* which a friend told him he must go to see. His curiosity outweighed his scruples and he did. He was amazed. The story began for the public when a guy called Bobby started college in upstate New York in 1980. Students began greeting him like an old friend and calling him Eddy. He'd dropped out a year before and Bobby was persuaded to get in touch with him. When they met there was no doubt the they were twins who had been adopted at birth by different families. They looked, talked and walked alike. It made newspaper headlines and before long they were contacted by another teen, David, who had the same birth date and adoption agency. The lively three were reunited and became a media sensation, a hit on the talk show circuit and were soon living it up in the club scene in New York City. They became inseparable as if making up for lost time and opened a restaurant in SoHo called Triplets.

Things began to go wrong. Bobby left the business after disagreements. In 1995 Eddy was taken to hospital with manic depression and committed suicide. Worse was to come. A journalist for the New Yorker discovered that a psychiatrist called Peter Neubauer had worked with a Jewish adoption agency in the city to study the nature versus nature question with twins separated at birth. The triplets had been part of that experiment and each one was placed in different sorts of families: working class, middle class, monied class. The findings had never been published and a good thing too, thought Arwyn. Hadn't there been enough experiments on twins, and Jewish ones at that?

Over the years many people had asked Arwyn what it was like being a twin. He could only answer that he knew nothing else - it was normal for him. But there was no doubt about it: being a twin could be a complicated business.

Martin had mentioned that he'd bumped into a cousin of the twins, Nora, and she'd like to see him. She was three or four years younger, but when young they were a great trio - building dens in the woods, damming streams, and getting up to all sorts of mischief. Nora was feisty and fearless, egging on the boys beyond their daring.

Her mother was a cousin of their father, or something like that. When they were young, she lived with her two older sisters on a farm on the other side of the hill. It was a menacing place, the gloomy old house with dark grey walls and small, murky windows. Its cheery name, Brynheulog, meant Sunnybank and seemed somehow to add to its sinisterness, so inappropriate was it. Arwyn found the set up forbidding and a little scary. His mother would speak of the farmstead and family in hushed tones, but not to him - only to certain grown-ups. In the way that children sense these things, he knew that Brynheulog held mysteries within its gloomy walls. Although he and Bren never spoke of it, he sensed his brother felt the same way, and they avoided going there if they could. They would climb their respective slopes of the Black Mountains and meet at places and times appointed by secret messages left in their own special place.

After their parents died, the sisters carried on farming, never married and rarely left the farm. They were good workers, and bought in help for the heavy stuff. The living got harder and smaller, but they wouldn't give up. It was only after the death of the older two that it came out that the oldest, Winnie, was not Nora's sister at all, but her mother. The fifteen year-old Winnie and *her* mother had hidden themselves away for months so they could carry out their plan, such was the shame of an illegitimate birth on the girl's family back in those days. When Nora was born she was presented to the outside world as Winnie's sister. And then, the family closed in on itself.

It was Arwyn's mother who told him all this shortly before her death. He didn't know who else knew, not even Bren, so it was never spoken of. But the reclusiveness, the atmosphere then made sense. Nora had made a brief appearance at the infamous party. She'd become dowdy and withdrawn. They'd exchanged but a few words, the customary wishes and thanks. So now he was curious to see her again, one last time.

Martin had said he hadn't seen her for years either - a bit of a recluse, was how he described her. She only came down to Crickhowell the other day to see the doctor. But she wanted to see Arwyn. From the way Martin spoke of her, it was clear that he did not know her story. It was as if people were to be blamed for shutting themselves away. But Arwyn couldn't wait to see her.

He asked Jac if he wanted to go for a ride over the mountains that afternoon, and he readily agreed. Arwyn was pleased - it would provide an opportunity for him to talk about his father now that he'd seen him or

ask questions if he needed to. But Arwyn also understood that he'd taken him there for another reason - to
act as his shield.

He rang Nora that morning.

'Hullo,' she said, as if she'd talked to him yesterday.
Yes, they could come that afternoon, for tea.

It was an enchanting drive through the winding lanes
that skirted the mountains and climbed the other side
up to Brynheulog. Arwyn followed them instinctively,
admiring the autumnal palette of the trees: vivid reds,
bronzes and golds. But his stomach churned as they
went through the bottom gate half off its hinges, and
up through the woods to catch the first glimpse of the
gable end of the forlorn house. It had barely changed,
except that the farm buildings were going to rack and
ruin. The roof of the old half-timbered barn sagged
and had collapsed in the middle, exposing the timbers.
Nature had reclaimed much of the yard and the path to
the side door was all but hidden by the wild grass.
Arwyn brushed it aside to let Jac through and then
gave a loud rap on the peeling paint of the side door.
The front door, as far as he could remember, was never used.

'Come in, come in,' croaked a voice within.

It opened into the kitchen. Nora got up from a rocking chair in front of the fire in the old black range, smoothing down her rather dishevelled clothing without making a noticeable difference. She waddled over to them. The room smelled musty and smokey.

'Good to see you, boy,' she said, and leaned up for a kiss.

'Hello, Nora,' said Arwyn.

'And here's young Jac. Duw, I haven't seen you since you were a twt.'

'No,' agreed Jac with a smile, but looked mystified.

'Come in and sit you down,' said Nora.

She shooed a cat from one of the scruffy old armchairs for Arwyn and pulled up a kitchen chair for Jac.

'Alright there, luv?'

'Yes, *I* am.'

The kitchen belonged to a world that was lost to Arwyn in all but memory. An old kettle was bubbling on the range, and a tin of paper spills stood on the hearth. There was a two-ring hotplate on the table next to the Belfast sink. It was clear that Nora spent all her time in this one room.

'And how *is* Bren,' she asked, turning to Arwyn.

He recounted the past few days, but didn't want to say too much in front of Jac. Nora read between the lines and nodded sadly, but then beamed at him.

'Why don't you go and have a sprwt outside, Jac?' she said. 'Do you remember the old place?'

'Yes, *I* do,' he said, but it was clear to Arwyn that he didn't.

He got up and gave his uncle a glance, as if for permission, which Arwyn granted in the form of an encouraging nod.

'I thought we might as well have a good chat, while you're here,' she said when he'd gone. 'So there's not much hope then, long-term?'

'It seems not. He was quite a bit better last night, but that's to be expected. Sally Mumford's daughter Shirley works there and she tells me what's going on.'

'Poor aul' Bren. And in our family too. Not usually our trouble.'

She eyed him narrowly.

'You got yourself checked out.'

'Not yet. But I'm feeling OK.'

'Aye, well….' and Nora left it hanging in the air.

The two chatted amiably on in front of the fire, catching up on old acquaintance and relations.

'I found the old family Bible at The Gro,' said Arwyn, 'and came across something strange.'

Nora nodded her interest, and Arwyn told her about the different birth years their mother had written.

She thought about it for a couple of moments, but it was enough to tell him that she knew of no secret, with an answer off-pat.

'It's bound to be a mistake, Ar. There couldn't possibly be a year's difference in you. People would have noticed. Talked. And why?'

Arwyn thought that her own family had kept secrets well enough, but didn't like to say.

'No, you were so obviously twins. Remember, I grew up with you.'

'I suppose you're right,' he said. 'But it was so unlike her to make a mistake like that.'

'She was a busy woman. Cut her some slack.'

She was right. She'd set his mind at rest.

'And you haven't thought fit to come and see us in all this while?' she asked with a mischievous smile.

Arwyn squirmed in his seat a little.

'Was it something to do with the party?'

He explained that that's what he had assumed all these years, but he'd talked it over with Bren and

Bren didn't blame him. There must be something else, but it wasn't clear what. He asked Nora if Bren had said anything to her.

'Lor' love you, I've barely seen Bren myself since the party. But I was at your mother's funeral. And you weren't.'

'You think that's what it was? Why he stopped making contact?'

'Well, think about it, Ar.'

'But I was away in Saudi Arabia. I left him a message explaining. He never got back.'

'Have you talked to him about it?'

'Well, no.'

'Maybe you should.'

Arwyn could certainly see the sense in this, and, as awkward as it might be for both of them, made up his mind to do it.

'But what about you?' he said. 'Don't you get lonely up here?'

'Me? No. Used to it.'

His eyes wandered round the room that time forgot. It was cluttered and dusty in places - the plants on the sill in front of the murky window, the stack of newspapers beside the armchair by the fire. But the oilcloth on the table at which they sat was clean, as was the sideboard with its china dogs, a shiny bottle of Old Grouse, half empty, a couple of glasses, and two plates covered with teacloths.

Nora got up with a grunt and went over to the sideboard. From the cupboard she produced cups, saucers, plates, cutlery and a pot of raspberry jam. She took the teacloths off to reveal doorstep cheese and pickle sandwiches and Welsh cakes. He offered to help but she waved him away, making small talk as she did so.

'You can go and call Jac in for tea,' she said, as if making some kind of concession to him.

Arwyn obeyed and felt the autumn chill as he opened the door, closing it again quickly to keep the heat in. He called out but there was no reply. He strolled down the yard and peered in the dilapidated cowshed. He suddenly became aware of the collapsing granary roof in the old building at an adjacent angle, and he shouted more insistently. Still there was no answer. He went around the other side of the house towards the orchard and there he found Jac, prodding into a water butt with a large twig.

'Jac, what are you doing?'

'A frog jumped in there.' said his nephew, and laughed.

'I was getting worried about you.'

Jac laughed again.

Arwyn wondered if Jac knew of his father's phobia of frogs (he looked it up once - it's called ranidaphobia). When they were about ten, Bren went screaming down the yard after he'd turned over some stones and one jumped out. A couple of years later he was thumbing through some kind of nature book and asked Arwyn to come over and turn the page because there was a full colour close-up of a frog. All three brothers had one specific phobia: for Arwyn it was spiders and for Will it had been snakes. Will had come across what can only have been grass snake when they were lugging hay bales and he had done the same screaming bat out of hell act as Bren had done with a frog. Arwyn remembered he learnt something that day, seeing his big, masterful, invincible brother running so scared. In some weird way, it had given him confidence. But where did these phobias fit into the nature versus nurture debate?

He roused himself from his thoughts and said, 'It's a good job your Dad isn't here,' and realised what a stupid thing it was to say before he'd finished the sentence.

Jac merely laughed.

'Come on, it's teatime,' said Arwyn.

Nora was pouring water from the steaming kettle on the range into a Brown Betty, and covered it with a crocheted cosy.

'Come on then. Sit yourselves down.'

She poured the tea and proffered the huge sandwiches. Jac seemed highly amused by the proceedings and watched Nora's every move. She took the whisky from the sideboard and motioned it to Arwyn.

'Fancy a bit of a winter warmer in your tea?' she asked.

Arwyn smiled.

'It's autumn, Nora.'

'Ah well, you can't be too careful,' and after she'd given him some, went over to make the same motion to Jac, but Arwyn caught her eye and gave the slightest shake of his head. Jac and strong drink did not mix. She shrugged and poured a hefty slug into her own cup.

Arwyn managed to get his mouth round one of the smaller corners of a sandwich and again Jac chuckled almost silently. Nora seemed not to notice. She was looking at Arwyn for approval.

'Homemade,' she said.

'The bread?'

'The pickle. Gave up cooking bread ages ago. Too much faff, and not much cheaper.'

'So how do you manage for groceries up here?'

'Ah well,' and here she perked up, 'I've still got my garden out the back. It's my pride and joy and gives me something to do. Jones delivers what I need. Don't bother much with meat any more. In fact I don't eat much at all. Do you?'

'Not as much as I used to, no.'

'But I do like doing my pickles and jams and soups and cakes and what have you. Carrot cake a speciality. Pity I didn't have any today.'

'Well, I can come again.' They looked at each other in surprise, then laughed.

'You could at that. It's a long time since I had visitors. It's doing me the power of good, hearing all your news from the outside world. But Ar…'

'What?'

'Don't feel too sorry for me.'

Arwyn realised he had been feeling sorry for her, finding her in this state of reclusion, friendless, love-less, living in her past. It was natural to believe that those near to us should have the same joys, the rich-ness of life that we do, he told himself. Maybe we are programmed to want the same for others as we want for ourselves. It seemed such a small life for such a big soul. But he could see that she was content with her home, her garden and a tot or two to help her through the day. And who was he to deny someone happiness?

'I'm not feeling sorry for you Nora, not any more anyway. I'm just remembering old times, is all. And I suppose it's always nice to see people being happy with friends and family. But I know where you're coming from. I can't blame you for cutting yourself off from people. I've done the same myself.'

'There weren't that many to cut myself from,' she said.

She saw them to the door. He noticed the whisky bottle was still on the table. Well good luck to her, is what he thought. Jac went ahead to the car.

'I probably won't make it down to see Bren,' she said.

'Well, if you change your mind…..'

'But remember me to him.'

She must have caught the sorrow in his eyes.

'I really am quite content, you know. I never really fitted in with others for, well, for reasons you probably know.'

Arwyn nodded gently.

'I was kept apart, and apart I must be now. I'm probably as happy now as I ever was. Apart from those times with you and Bren. What did we used to call ourselves? The Intrepid Trio? Something like that?'

Arwyn had forgotten.

'Yes,' he said, 'the Intrepid Trio.'

'I always felt I belonged with you two. You're going to miss him terribly.'

'I know,' he could only agree. '

'Talk to him.'

'I will, Nora, I promise. I'd better be off, now.'

Jac was honking the horn and laughing. Arwyn bent down and pecked her on the cheek.

Seeing Nora had unnerved Arwyn more so than with Bren in some ways. He supposed it was because Bren had been so much a part of his life, whereas Nora had rekindled memories that were extinguished, times when he too was happy some seventy years before. Strangely enough, he hadn't thought out in words what it would be like when that part of him was gone. As they drove back in the deepening dusk, he now wondered what he would do. Could he go back to the flat in Marylebone Lane, saying goodbye to all this as he had before? There was a time, in his youth, when one of his ambitions was to outlive Bren. Now, all of a sudden, the thought of being the last of his brothers to go was almost too much to bear.

'What you thinking?' asked Jac, who didn't like long silences.

'Oh, nothing much,' said his uncle.

11.A matter of time

Arwyn dropped Jac off and he went happily into the house. He'd asked if he wanted to come and see his father but Jac had said, 'No, I'm alright.'

As he drove down the long straight stretch towards Abergavenny, Arwyn suddenly thought he'd forgotten Bren's shaving things. He turned around in the entrance to Nevill Hall Hospital, and drove almost back to Crickhowell before he remembered that they were still in the back of the car. His dwindling memory was the most frightening thing about growing old, he thought. He'd long been used to going into his bedroom to get something only to find that by the time he got there he'd forgotten what he was he wanted. But more and more recently he was losing track of the thread of time running through the day. Perhaps it was for the best in some ways, as it left more room for the goodness, like the times with Nora, that came shining through ever more strongly.

Shirley was on the reception desk.

'And how's the patient this evening?' he asked, aware of how clichéd this sounded. She gave him a warm smile, and walked him to Bren's room.

'About the same. He seems quite happy in himself. He's looking forward to seeing you, if only for the shave.'

'Oh, he's told you about that, has he?'

'Oh, yes. No secrets here.'

'Talking of which, everyone I see asks me, well, how long he's got, to put it bluntly.'

'There's still no way of telling,' said Shirley after a deep breath. 'The morphine keeps the pain at bay and his spirits up. There's not much more we can do for him. It's just a matter of time. But I shouldn't be telling you all this. It should really come from the doctor.'

'Yes, Martin's been talking to her in the daytime. As you say, just a matter of time.'

She left him just before they came to his room, and he entered it with a more peaceful frame of mind than he had in the previous visits. Bren, he thought, looked a little weaker, but his withered face showed a spark of expectancy that he had not seen before. Perhaps it was the thought of the shave.

'What time d'you call this?' said Bren with an air of mischief.

Arwyn was sure that no set time had been mentioned.

'I call it as soon as I could bloody well get here. What time do you call it? Moany o'clock?'

Bren gave the biggest smile Arwyn had so far seen.

'I've brought the shaving kit,' he said.

'Oh thanks. But there's plenty of time for that. Here, have a seat. Tell me what you know.'

This time, at least, he had some news of something he thought Bren would be interested in. He said he'd been up to see Nora.

'Nora? Good God. Haven't see her for years. How is the old gal?'

He described the visit to Brynheulog. Bren listened thoughtfully, with interest. Arwyn couldn't quite bring himself yet to broach the subject of his missing their mother's funeral.

'It's funny she said that to you, that she's content,' he said when Arwyn had finished.

'Yes, well, I suppose it depends on what you've had before.'

'We did have some good times. Remember when we'd seen that film about Gladys Aylward in China before the War. What was it called again?'

'The Inn of the Sixth Happiness.'

'The Inn of the Sixth Happiness,' confirmed Bren. 'We wanted to create the scene when she leads the orphans to safety across the mountains.'

'*Singing Knick-Knack Paddywhack, Give a Dog a Bone.*'

'*This old man came rolling home,*' sang Bren. And he chuckled. 'Funny old song. Wonder what it meant.'

'I'll look it up,' said Arwyn.

'So we took her up the mountain and we had to lay flat on the ground every time the Japanese bombers came over.'

He was lost in the memory for a few moments. It seemed a happy one.

'I don't think she enjoyed it very much,' he said.

'She remembers them as happy times too.'

'And I don't think her parents were best pleased.'

'Perhaps they never had much to be pleased about.'

'No,' said Bren.

They were both finding the flow of conversation easier now, and Arwyn told him about seeing Kitty the other day. Again, Bren seemed to delight in recalling his younger days - how beautiful and vivacious she was, how she entranced them all.

'It's horrible to think of her sitting there, drifting in and out of reality,' he said.

'She seemed happy enough too.'

'Maybe, but it's the worst thing I can think of. I'd rather go quickly, when the time comes.'

It was the first time either of them had acknowledged that his end might be near. Bren seemed relieved to be able to talk about it, and got into his stride. He wasn't afraid, he said, but this dying business was tedious. He wanted a quick end, as he knew he could never go back to any kind of normal life. When you got to this state of decay, he said, the thought of eternal rest was quite attractive. Not that he had a death wish.

Arwyn knew what he meant. The Fflints had never been particularly religious. The little local chapel was more of a social bond than anything else. His parents enjoyed a good funeral and the Harvest Festival was a highlight of the calendar.

Arwyn asked him what he thought was after life. Bren said simply: 'Dust to dust.' Now they were talking so freely and easily, Arwyn felt he could ask some of the questions that had been niggling him of late but which he hadn't had the heart to broach. He wanted to know if Bren had made any funeral arrangements.

'Oh, nothing fancy. One of these baskets will do me fine. And now there's a burial ground on the lower slopes of the Blorenge, overlooking Llwyn Onn. I think I'll go there. It's all in my will. Martin's got a copy. It's all taken care of. And some money behind the bar at The Dragon for a good knees-up. Like Dad did.'

'So you're not fussed about going in the family plot in the cemetery?'

'I can't really get worked up about that, Ar. What about you?'

'I feel the same way, really. I don't really care about what happens when I'm gone. Perhaps I should. I haven't put anything in my will because I didn't care enough about it one way or the other. Cremation at Golder's Green, I suppose. There's quite a bit for Jac.'

'The boy's going to be alright. How's he doing?' asked Bren.

While the going was good and the two brothers seemed to be getting on so well, Arwyn related the events of - when was it, yesterday morning? - when he disappeared.

'Ay well, he does do that now and again, when he wants to think about something. Don't worry about it. It wasn't your fault. He'll tell you if he wants to know anything.'

'Well, I'm just worried that he might go AWOL again and get himself into trouble.'

'What trouble?'

'I don't know. That's the trouble.'

'Oh, he can look after himself. Thank God.'

Arwyn said he'd given him the chance to come and see his father, but he just kept saying he was alright. 'That means he is,' said Bren.

'Do you think he understands what's happening to you?'

'In his own way, yes. He's lost loved ones before, remember. Mam for example. Oddly enough, he seems to take it in his stride. He behaved remarkably well at her funeral.'

Was that a little dig?

'Do you tell him that he'll see you again in Heaven?'

'No, I don't want to lie to him. He gets some of that in Llandeilo, I think. I just tell him I'm going for a good rest. I think behind it all is the fact that he doesn't want to see me like this, going downhill. He wants to remember me as I used to be.'

The twins sat in silence for a minute or two, each lost in his own thoughts.

'Come on,' said Bren finally, 'time for my shave.'

Arwyn jumped to it, positioned the bed table near Bren's chin and tied a towel round his neck. He filled a bowl with water as hot as his hands could stand, soaked a flannel in it, wrapped it round his stubble and left it a few minutes. He then smothered it in moisturiser. Bren was clearly enjoying the whole ritual and had set aside his initial misgivings about the pampering. He lathered him in gel, switched on the vibrating razor and gently scraped the hair away.

Arwyn felt emboldened to further their newfound openness and intimacy. He wanted to get the party business out of the way once and for all.

'You know, I'd always thought we'd stopped speaking after that business with Annie at our fiftieth.'

He wiped down Bren's face with the flannel, and dried it off with the towel.

'Well, I sort of could see why you invited her. You couldn't have predicted how she'd behave, I suppose. Meryl was pretty cut up by it, of course, and thought you'd masterminded the whole thing in some strange way of getting at her.'

'What did you say?'

'I told her not to be so daft. She'd always resented you a little for keeping in touch with Annie after we married. I suppose there was a bit of jealousy there. But in time Meryl came to see that there was nothing malicious in it on your part. '

'So you didn't really hold it against me?'

'I got over it.'

Arwyn pressed on. He told him what Nora had said, that Bren had never forgiven him for not coming to their mother's funeral.

'Ah, well, that was a bit off,' said Bren. 'You know what they're like for funerals around here.'

'I did try to let you know,' said Arwyn. 'That I was in Saudi Arabia at the time and there was no way of getting back. Not it time, anyway. I was embedded.'

'I know what that feels like,' said Bren with a ghost of a chuckle.

'I mean with the army - with the allied forces after Iraq invaded Kuwait. If you're embedded as a journalist in a war zone you have to more or less have to sign up to the military and obey the rules. You can't just pack up your kitbag, smile and wave bye-bye.'

'Well, how did you try to get hold of me?'

Both were now beginning to raise their voices.

'Well, they'd let me know she'd died from the office in London......'

'Well, yes. I rang them up.'

'And then I managed to get an international call through and left a message on your answering machine.'

'Did you?' said Bren. 'Well, I was never much good with them damn things. Perhaps it got deleted by mistake.'

Bren looked at his brother and seemed to find a look of confusion in his brother's eye.

'Don't you believe me?' he asked.

'Do you believe you?'

'Yes, I do,' said Bren. 'I'm telling you I never got that message.

'The curse of modern communication,' said Arwyn.

The two were quiet for a few moment while they chewed all this over.

'You could have written,' said Bren at last.

'Yes, I could have. And I meant to. But I got caught up in things. It wasn't easy out there, you know. Every day was a fight for survival, as well as getting all the filming done in very difficult circumstances. I'm sure I was just as upset as you about not being there. I felt very badly. But there was nothing I could do.'

Both twins had calmed down by now. Bren looked at his brother searchingly for a moment.

'Maybe. I was angry with you at the time, and so was everyone else. It was saving face for you that was the hardest - you know, answering everyone when they asked why you weren't there. I didn't know my-self and felt I had to make excuses for you.'

Bren paused a while to catch his breath. He seemed keen to talk now.

"But you know how I feel about the trappings and conventions. It's not how you go that matters, it's how you lived. And I suppose deep down I did understand that you would have come if you could. You were with her when she had the stroke.'

Arwyn didn't admit that he'd forgotten that bit, but now the memories came back. Perhaps he'd blanked it out. He was surprised to hear his brother say after all this time that he understood. He'd always thought that no-one had. And now he realised he'd lived with the guilt for so many years, buried deep down some-where. But if that were so, that can't have been the only cause of their long estrangement either, he rea-soned to himself.

'What was it then?' he asked, almost as much of himself as of Bren. 'What was it that's kept us apart for all of these years? We may as well have it out once and for all, now with our hair down. Thank God we've still got some.'

Bren sighed.

'Not now, Ar. I'm tired. It takes it out of me, all this talk. But I think it's doing me good as well. We'll have another go tomorrow. It was good to see you. Thanks for the shave. It's been the highlight of my twilight,' and he gave one of his wheezy half chuckles.

'You've been working on that one,' said Arwyn.

'Nothing much else to do.'

And with that, Bren slumped back against the pillows. Arwyn could see he was exhausted, and he had no choice but to leave him. He put his hand on his shoulder and squeezed it.

'See you tomorrow, then.'

'See you tomorrow.'

12.A faraway farewell

Nell had had a stroke the day after their party. Bren found her lying at the bottom of the stairs. It was all coming back to Arwyn. Somehow the passing years had distorted his memory, so in his own mind she'd had the stroke after he'd left for London, and he'd never seen her again.

Nell wouldn't hear of moving out of Llwyn Onn after their father died, and as she got more and more infirm. Her sons and their families begged her, and even went so far as half-plotting to kidnap her.

She'd made them swear years before that they'd never put her in an old folks home. She and her ilk associated it with the workhouse, as had their father - a shameful fate worse than death. When she was well into her eighties, and struggling alone in the rambling farmhouse, Will and Bren had found a place in Crickhowell, a little sheltered ground floor flat that they could rent cheaply from the council. There was even an old neighbour she knew quite well living in the upstairs flat. The brothers were pleased with themselves that they'd found a solution for her and them: Will and Bren between them had been keeping a close eye on her and saw to all her needs - shopping, the doctors and the rest of it. They took it in turns to go up and make her breakfast, but in fact the food was ready and waiting when they got there. Meryl went to give her her bath. It would be easier down in the town, they all said. Arwyn had even rung her a couple of times from the West Bank or Saudi Arabia or wherever he was to beg her to go, but she wouldn't hear of it.

The day before the party Arwyn arrived from London and went to Llwyn Onn to stay with her. She didn't move much from her chair in the living room, watching snooker on the TV. It had always been a very cold room but now it was like an oven, with both the radiators and two bars of the electric fire on, and she kept a thick woollen shawl around her shoulders. Oh, I don't feel the cold, she'd say. It wasn't surprising. Someone had put a thermometer just inside the door, and when Arwyn went in he furtively turned the thermostat right down from the eighty something and switched off the electric fire. He simply couldn't stand sitting there with her in such a heat. Oddly, though, the next morning the thermostat was back in its customary position and the temperature was back up in the eighties, even though his mother claimed not to know how it worked.

She told him she worried about the heating bills - as well she might, he thought. But he said: 'Mam, you have three sons. You needn't ever bother yourself about things like that.' They knew that their father had left her comfortably off, and of course she valued her independence.

It had just been assumed that Nell would come to the twins' party, but that morning she told Arwyn she didn't feel up to it.

'You young 'uns go enjoy yourselves,' she'd said as she used to when they were, in fact, young. 'I'm better off here.'

Arwyn was genuinely disappointed but she waved aside his protests.

'I don't want to be a nuisance,' she'd said, in that unconvincing martyred air she sometimes affected to get her own way.

'Well, you're being a bloody nuisance now,' Arwyn had said.

It was Meryl who later pointed out that it might have been because she was worried about frequent trips to the toilet. They'd noticed when they fetched her for Sunday dinner that she didn't drink anything. She had trouble getting up to their bathroom, as their stairs were steep and had no handrails. So it was in vain that Meryl urged her to drink more water, as it was good for the system. And it was true that Nell had never been one for pubs, even less so now that the general hubbub drowned out what people were saying to her. She'd only ever gone in one on those Sunday evening jaunts across the border for their father to find one that was open. At one point Meryl had suggested they convert one of the downstairs rooms of the farmhouse into an en suite bedroom. The three brothers agreed to pick up the cost, but Nell wasn't keen and it came to nothing.

The morning after the party, Arwyn had been woken by a hammering on his door about ten o'clock. It was Bren. He'd found their mother lying on the floor in the hall. Apparently she'd got up early and gone down to make a cup of tea, but fell and had lain there for two or three hours, unable to move. Bren's face was set in that way that showed how furious he was that Arwyn was sleeping off his hangover when he could have got to her earlier.

They made her as comfortable as possible, putting a pillow under her head, squeezing cushions under her back at which she gave a small squeak of pain, and covering her with a quilt. Bren said they should take her to Nevill Hall in the back of the Land Rover but thought the better of it when Arwyn just snorted. He called an ambulance and there was the usual faff in giving directions in a way they could understand. It took them quite a while.

Nell seemed quite peaceful on the floor, and was even smiling weakly. She could speak in short whispers and kept saying she was fine, as if it was perfectly normal to be lying on the hall floor at ten thirty in the morning. Bren made a cup of sugary tea and she managed to take a couple of sips when they put another pillow under her head, but even though she said it was lovely and she felt better, they could tell she was wincing in pain.

Arwyn went in the ambulance with her, telling Bren to get on with his work which he seemed ready to do. It was nerve-wracking in triage in the hospital: for a long while the nurse couldn't get the needle into the spidery purple veins in her hands for the canular. Nell was still serene, but Arwyn could hardly watch. By this time her hand was covered in blood and the nurse started trying the other.

'What they doing now?' asked Nell.

'He's going to lacerate your other hand now, Mam,' said Arwyn, and when the poor nurse who was trying his best shot him a look of pure frustration, Arwyn could have bitten his tongue to stop it being so quick.

It was managed after several attempts and she was moved into a four-berth ward. She said she was tired and wanted to sleep so Arwyn left her. Later that afternoon they rang to confirm she'd had a stroke and was being transferred to the little cottage hospital in Crickhowell, long since gone, the next day.

Bren insisted on going to Nevill Hall to bring her back in the ambulance, so the other two brothers had to leave him to it. The three of them gathered round Nell's bed early in the evening. She was peaceful but weak, and couldn't say much, but kept assuring them that she was fine and not to fuss. Bren sat at her bedside holding her hand and kept up a constant chattering of small talk. Arwyn sat the other side of the bed and chipped in now and again. Will, though, was silent. He sat stiffly in a chair by the far wall, visibly shaken and upset. He was considered in the family as the toughest of them all, a farmer through and through who liked mixing with his own kind and spurned the bright lights of Abergavenny and Newport, preferring the small country pubs around. But now, it was as if his mother's illness had somehow defeated him, knocked all the swagger out of him.

Nell closed her eyes and slumped back against the pillow. It was hard to tell if she'd fallen asleep or lost consciousness or……. Bren leant forward and put his ear to her mouth.

'She's breathing,' he said. 'It's weak, but I can feel her breath.' The others let out theirs. He went outside and found the nurse Sally, mother of Shirley who was nursing him now. She bustled in, greeted them cheerfully and fussed around Nell, taking her pulse and temperature and adjusting the drip and whatnot.

'She's just drifted out of consciousness,' she said, straightening up and smoothing down her uniform. 'It's probably not for long and it might happen from time to time.'

Bren announced he wanted to stay the night with his mother. The only other bed in the little ward was empty and he asked if he could sleep there. She shrugged as if to say why not and said she would see what she could do. Bren took up his position by the head of the bed, stroked her hand and talked.

Will and Arwyn went outside for a cigarette.

'I don't know how Bren can keep on wittering away like that,' said Will, looking away up into the Black Mountains. 'I don't know what to say. Wind's sharp,' and he brushed his eye as if flicking away a speck of dirt.

'I don't think it matters very much. Sally told him to keep on talking even if she didn't seem to be conscious. You never know what's going in.'

When they went back, Sally had laid out a woman's nightie on the spare bed, and put a little bunch of violets on the bedside cabinet. Bren was still holding Nell's hand, and looked around at them somewhat sheepishly.

'Sally says it's OK for me to stay overnight,' he said. 'Meryl will come early tomorrow so I can go home for some breakfast.'

It was clear he was thinking of some kind of shift system so Nell wouldn't be alone. He looked up at Arwyn expectantly.

'Oh, yes, and I could come down after dinner to relieve Meryl,' he said, although he couldn't see that a round-the-clock vigil was strictly necessary. Sally had their numbers and had assured them that they'd keep a close eye on her and phone them if need be. They in their turn looked at Will but he seemed to be staring intently out of the window.

'Ah, well, we can take it from there,' sighed Bren.

He came up to the farm after breakfast the next morning. Arwyn was just finishing off his - two rounds of bread fried on one side in butter - fried piecies, they'd called them as kids when this was their favourite morning meal - and two runny fried eggs, with a pinch of salt on the yolks. As he was making it he wondered what had got into him to resort to this comfort food, but then of course he realised.

Bren sat down at the kitchen table, twiddling his cap and looking drained.

'Well, how is she?' said Arwyn as he made him a mug of coffee and set it before him.

'About the same. She was awake and with it when I left her, but weak. Still cheerful, though.'

Arwyn nodded and joined him at the table.

'She's asking for Will.'

'Oh. He seems pretty upset.'

'Well, we're all upset,' snapped Bren.

'Of course. In our different ways.'

Bren looked up at him sharply.

'What did you tell her?' asked Arwyn.

'That he'd be down to see her soon, of course.'

When Arwyn was driving down the farm lane for his shift at the hospital later that day he met Will coming up on the tractor. They both had to drive up a little

way into the ditches to pass. As they did so, Arwyn
wound his window down.

'Well, how is she?' asked Will.

'About the same. She's asking where you are.'

Will started sniffling gently, choking it back.

'Don't make me go there, Ar. I'd only get upset and
that would upset her and that would do neither of us
any good.'

'You may not get many more chances,' said his
brother. 'Just think about it.'

'Aye. alright,' said Will, and drove off.

As he was walking from the car he'd hired in London up the steps into the little hospital, Meryl was
coming out, still tight-lipped from the incident at the
party.

'Well, I've done my bit,' she said. 'It's up to you
boys now. I saw my mother through it - I don't want
to go through it again.'

'That's fine, Meryl. Thanks for staying with her.'

She gave a slight shake of her head as if to say no
thanks were called for.

'What about Will? Bren said he's pretty shaken up.'

'I met him on the lane. I don't think he's up to coming to see her just yet.'

Meryl thrust her chin out with a tut.

'Well, as I say, it's up to you boys now,' and she walked briskly to her car. At the time, he thought she'd got it in for him because of what happened at the party.

Nell, he thought, looked frailer and her breathing was heavier, but she still looked serene enough. He tried to keep up the conversation, but she could only contribute in short bursts. He found that she responded best if he asked her questions about the past. Had Will been born at home? Yes, babies were in those days before the War, and before the National Health. Her Auntie Jeannie was a midwife. What about him and Bren? No, because they were twins. She'd had them here, in the cottage hospital.

Bren appeared after tea, when Nell was asleep. He asked in a whisper if there'd been any sign of Will. Arwyn whispered back about the encounter on the lane.

'If you go back now, do you think you could come back by bedtime and stay with her?'

'Do you think that's necessary? Sally's on tonight and you know how good she is.'

'It isn't asking much,' he said.

When he got back to the farm, he found Meryl there. She'd taken the dirty clothes from his room and washed them and ironed them. She was stacking them neatly on a chair by the kitchen table and looked as if she'd been caught in the act of something underhand.

'I'm only doing it because your Mam's sick,' she said, as if he might think it was an act of random kindness.

He thanked her as profusely as he thought she would want, and then she asked if he wanted her to make him some supper. He thanked her again and said he could see to himself.

'Oh well, if you're sure.'

He got back to the hospital at about half past ten. Sally was tidying Nell's bed as Bren looked on.

'I've brought some clean pyjamas, Sally, so there's no need for a nightie tonight.'

Nell was asleep and he turned in shortly too, but couldn't get to sleep. Sally came in about two o'clock. 'Look, why don't you get off,' she said. 'I can manage here. There's nothing you can do, anyway. I'll cover for you with Bren.'

So feeling guilty, but desperate for sleep, he couldn't resist taking her at her word and slinking away.

The phone call from London came the next morning just after nine. They couldn't put off the Saudi Arabia trip any longer. They'd have to leave tomorrow - all the arrangements were made. They'd be filming for two weeks.

Arwyn was torn and he felt slightly sick. The programme had been a long time in the planning, getting all the permissions, army embedding and so on, and there was no telling how long he would be needed here anyway. Almost on automatic pilot he packed his small bag as he had dozens of times before and checked that everything was in order around the house. As he was closing the door, Bren drove into the yard and gave a look of incredulity when he saw the bag.

'You off?'

Arwyn explained the situation, that he really had no choice, it was in his contract.

'I'll be back in a couple of weeks,' he said.

Bren just walked off without a word. Arwyn stood staring after him for a minute or two, but then jumped decisively into the car.

He called in at the hospital, of course. Nell roused slightly.

'I've got to go back to London for work, Mam,' - he didn't go into the whole Saudi Arabia trip - ' but I'll be back soon. You'll be better then and we'll have a good old catch-up.'

He wanted to linger, to chat a while, but Nell said, 'Off you go then.'

He lingered at their parting, holding the door open.

'Goodbye love.'

She'd never said that to him before. It was always 'Be seeing you, love.'

She knew. She died three days later.

13.The final reckoning?

In the cosy cottage at The Gro, Alwyn lay awake thinking of his mother, of Kitty, Nora and Bren. It was hard to take a stance on this dying business. It was all very well for Dylan Thomas to urge us not to go gentle into that good night, but it was pretty grim in death's waiting room. All four of them were content enough in different ways, and ready to meet the end. He believed that life was a part that had to be played out until the final curtain call, while at the same time fully supporting the right of someone suffering terminally to chose when to go. There was no easy way out. He thought too of Robbie, a friend of his third wife, Maxine. She and her husband had left London in their retirement and bought their dream cottage in Dorset, or so they thought. When he died she was alone - they had no children and Robbie had fallen out with her only near relation her brother. She developed cancer and left the little village by the sea without a word to a soul. Somehow Maxine found out that she'd gone to Switzerland, where they'd lived for a couple of years a while back. It didn't take long to work out that she'd gone for easy access to Dignitas. Maxine remembered her talking about Montreux, and as she was half French rang every clinic around to find her and wouldn't take non for an answer. When they did track her down, Robbie was not best pleased, and told them not to come and visit, as she wanted to be alone in her misery. Maxine wouldn't be put off, and took Arwyn for a weekend break, so Robbie didn't have much choice but to see them. They took her out for lunch in a restaurant garden bordering the lake. She liked a glass of wine or two, or three…. It turned out that she wanted to talk about Dignitas, but it was frowned on in the clinic. Once she found she could discuss it freely with them, she perked up consider- ably. She saw it as her last act of independence.

When they went to see her the next day, a woman in a white coat introduced herself as the head of the clinic and called them into her office and asked if they'd given her wine. Of course, they said, they all had some with their lunch. They were not to give her more than a glass of wine, said the woman. She'd become difficult with staff afterwards. She just helped herself, they said. Robbie was a difficult woman to say no to.

Maxine paid her two other visits, taking her out on the lake steamer or up on the mountain railway. In the end, Robbie died without having to resort to Dignitas. There was no easy way out, although she did spend her last few weeks having little adventures that she could not have foreseen.

But is it enough just to be, as one usually is towards the end. No plans, projects, adventures, loves? It's then that life can seem so totally pointless. But maybe it's only then that we can fully appreciate the essence of being, the joy of life. Arwyn seemed to change his ideas all the time on this. What then was his true view? What would it be at his last breath?

When he got back from the hospital after the discussion about their mother's funeral, he found Jac and Martin toiling over a five hundred piece jigsaw of pub signs. He joined in as best as his weakened eyesight allowed.

He told Jac he'd seen his father and they'd had a nice chat.

Jac merely smiled and nodded, wrapped up in the puzzle.

'When do you want to go to see Dad?' Martin asked him.

'When he's better,' said Jac, slotting a lock of the Marquis of Granby's hair into place.

Martin and Arwyn exchanged glances.

'He may not get better, Jac,' said Martin gently.

'I know,' said Jac simply.

After breakfast the next morning, Arwyn took a stroll down to the village shop to get a couple of odds and ends that Sioned needed, ignoring her protests that it would take her five minutes in the car. Jac was still busy with the pub signs.

Arwyn had been annoyed and intrigued by the hostility of the grocer: it went beyond the general suspicion and coldness of some of the other locals. It was the way round here to chat away in the shops. He remembered keeping this up when he went to university in London but people would look at you as if you were mad. Then when he came back in the holidays, people in Crickhowell took offence if he walked into a shop without saying hello and making small talk.

He'd learnt that his name was Rob Jones, and that his parents had kept the shop before him. Arwyn just about remembered them, but if the rude grocer was about fifty, he'd have been twenty at the time of the party and their mother's stroke. He had no recollection of him. He'd been in the shop a couple of times, only to be met with the same surly silence. So it was with some misgivings that he pushed open the door to the sound of the tinkling bell, but he was determined somehow to get to the bottom of it.

'Hello. Nice day,' he said cheerfully as his plan of attack. He couldn't tell whether there was the slightest nod or not. He picked up a couple of items from the shelves and took them over to the counter.

'Oh, and I'd like a book of stamps please - six second class.' The man sighed and stomped off to the Post Office side as if he'd been asked to produce a unicorn horn.

'Excuse me for asking you,' said Arwyn, 'but have I done anything to offend you?'

The man merely stared at him for a few moments. Arwyn stared back, seeing if he could discern in this old grouch any sign of the twenty year-old he must have been the last time their paths crossed. And by giving him a head of hair, paring down the jowls and even endowing him with at least a polite smile, it suddenly came to him: they had had a conversation that weekend. Arwyn just hadn't had the slightest inkling that they were the same man.

He'd started off conversationally enough, that time, chatting about the weather, of course, and then recognising him as Bren's brother. He'd heard about the party, inevitably, and wished them a happy one.

'And where do you live, yourself?' he'd asked.

'London.'

'Suppose someone has to.'

'Oh, I love it.'

'What, with all them foreigners?'

'Especially with all them foreigners.'

Arwyn went on to mention some of the great things about living in a vibrant multi-cultural city. This merely provoked the young Ron Jones into a full-scale racist rant which Arwyn did his utmost to interrupt and counter but he was no match for the vitriol pouring out of that mouth. In the end he'd picked up whatever he'd come in for and left.

'Anything else?' the old Ron said now, ignoring Arwyn's question.

Arwyn thought about taking him to task. But it was so many years ago and he asked himself what was the use. So he wished him a good day and walked out of the shop. As he made his way towards The Gro lane, he spotted Mary Upper Bryn pull up in a rather battered Vauxhall, a diesel by the sound of it. She got out with an old string shopping bag and they exchanged the customary pleasantries, and she asked after Bren. Arwyn in turn told her about Ron Jones' attitude towards him.

'Ah well, I wouldn't have any more to do with him than you can help. Nasty customer, he is.'

Arwyn sensed that she knew more than she was letting on.

'Any particular reason for you to say that?'

Mary, a gentle soul, became flustered.

'Please, Mary, it's been really bothering me what he's got against me.

'Well, I don't know…… I don't want to stir up trouble. But it's just that…..what you said then about the row you had….. Well, it makes sense.'

'What does? Come on, Mary.'

She took a decision.

'I expect you've heard about the rumour, about you and your…..wife?'

'That I killed her?'

'Yes. I didn't believe a word of it, of course. Not of you. But it was Ron Jones who started it, right enough.'

'What?'

'He's the source of all the gossip round here. He's known for it. I only go in there myself when I need something from the Post Office. He must have borne a grudge against you all that time and saw his chance when….'

'When my wife was killed?'

'Yes.'

'I've got a good mind to go back in there and have it out with him.'

'Don't Arwyn. He's not worth it. And he's got a ter- rible temper on him. He could do you serious harm.

'Maybe you're right.'

'Just focus on your brother. No-one believed him anyway.'

'It's funny you say that. You know when me and Jac came up to see you the other day. I thought that Geraint was, well, a bit off with me.'

'Oh, take no notice of him. He's a grumpy old bugger sometimes. Pardon my French. I think he was just sore that you hadn't been near the place for so long. He used to love you and Bren coming up when you were younger. He's sad about Bren too. You going to be round here for long?'

'I might go back to London for a while to sort a few things out. But I could come back.'

'Well, be sure to come up and see us. I'll sort out.'

They said their goodbyes. For all that he'd been enjoying his new-found sense of peace and purpose here, it was the tongue-wagging, head-shaking judging of other people that he just couldn't stomach. Thank God they didn't tweet much around here, the older ones at least, otherwise he would have been tried in the court of public opinion. In London you could find your own niche without anyone knowing or caring. And walking up the lane, Arwyn realised he'd said out loud something he hadn't even told himself - that he would probably come back here. It was true that he'd now begun to worry about his blood pressure pills. He could go up for a few days. Then it struck him that this is what happened the last time he was here: he left thinking he'd see his mother again and he never did. Surely history wouldn't repeat itself with Bren? That would be the cruellest blow.

But now the seed was planted, it began to grow. Sitting at the kitchen table after supper, when Jac was up in his room watching a film, he mentioned his plan to Martin and Sioned. He noticed them exchange quick, stealthy looks.

'We've been wondering how long you'd stick around,' said Martin, and Arwyn felt it made him sound like a feckless drifter. He explained the position with his blood pressure pills.

'Well then, yes, you need to get that sorted out,' said Sioned. 'But Martin and me have been thinking - why don't you move back here, at least for a while. What's to keep you in London?'

'Well, my friends, my habits, my life. Although it must be said that old friends are getting fewer and farther between. Some people seem to think I need to be rescued from Sodom and Gomorrah. But I'm happy there. And I'm a bit of a stranger here, if truth be told.'

'Well, there's always a home for you here, for as long as you like,' said Martin with a resigned shrug as if to say there was little more to be said on the matter.

Arwyn thanked them, and indeed he was immensely grateful, but he also resented being pressurised into doing something. Until quite recently he'd had no time for old people clinging stubbornly to their homes, instead of going to a place where they could be looked after in comfort and relieve the burden on their families. He'd always thought that he'd quite like some kind of nursing home to see him out. A few years back he and a few hack pals had joked about buying a big old house between them and hiring staff to look after them. As long as there were cards and wine. The idea started to become more and more attractive and so they took it more seriously. But nothing ever came of it. He still sometimes asked himself if he wouldn't like a comfortable billet with room service laid on. But his answer was always; Not yet. So now he knew how the old folks felt.

'I'll go back to London for a few days,' he said. 'And then we'll see.'

Arwyn got his coat for the trip to Newport.

'Best of luck,' said Martin, 'or whatever you say in the circumstances.'

He and Sioned had been to see Bren that afternoon, and found him not so good. They were going to give him more morphine and review his medication to see if they could make him more comfortable. Arwyn was eager to tell him that he and their mother had said their final goodbyes. Perhaps it would help further diminish the gulf that had existed between them.

Bren was quiet, but peaceful. Arwyn took out the shaving things but Bren said he didn't quite feel up to it tonight. Arwyn was disappointed. In a strange kind of way, it had become the highlight of his day, for both of them, by all appearances. So instead he described the final moments with Nell.

'So you see, we did say our goodbyes, after all.'

'Well, as I said, I didn't really hold that against you, not for all these years, although I was disappointed at the time.'

'And it wasn't the thing with Annie, you've told me that. So let's have it out Bren, here and now. Why did we waste those decades?'

'Takes two, remember.'

'Yes, but I thought you'd blown me out.'

'Blown you out? That's what they say these days, is it?'

'I thought you didn't want anything more to do with me. I always meant to get in touch to clear the air but, I don't know - I was busy, kept putting it off, every-day things got in the way and then months became years and then time itself became the thing, the thing between us. Know what I mean?

'Aye. Aye.'

There was a silence. It was Arwyn who broke it.

'And I thought you were ashamed of me.'

'Good God, Ar, never that. We may have had our ups and downs but.......'

'What was it then?'

Bren was silent for quite some time. Arwyn couldn't tell if he was thinking, or tiring, or deciding.

'Well one thing that has really stuck in my craw was that you cut yourself off from Jac. You two were always so close when he was growing up. Afterwards he used to ask about you a lot. But then he stopped.'

'I didn't go to see him, that's true, but we did keep in touch.'

'What? How......when?'

'A few years ago now. Must have been when he got his mobile phone. He rang me out of the blue one day - he'd got my number from Martin. Then he'd ring me from time to time, and asked me to ring him.'

'He never let on. What did you talk about?'

'This and that, you know. What he was doing. He kept tabs on me. Saw me on the telly sometimes.'

'Duw, Duw,' said Bren. He seemed amazed and said he'd never had an inkling of it. Arwyn for his part had been grateful for this relationship and it had never entered his head that he should let Bren know. Besides, he realised now, he must have just assumed that Jac would tell him - yet more proof that Bren wanted nothing to do with his twin. And so the resentment had grown and grown.

'Still, you could have come to see him, or gone to Llandeilo if you didn't want to see me.'

'Yes, you're right, I could have and should have. I see that now.'

By now every possible root cause of their mutual silence had turned out to be false. After sitting for a couple of minutes, with neither of them finding anything to say, Arwyn said as much to Bren. He nodded his head slowly, and said he was tired, as a cue for his brother to leave.

'Till tomorrow then,' said Arwyn, getting up from his chair with a little grunt.

'Aye. And Arwyn....'

Arwyn closed slightly the door he'd just opened. 'Think about your own part in this whole business.' Arwyn did think, on the way back and noticed he was driving somewhat fast and erratically. He adjusted his speed. He could easily have come off the dangerous corner just the other side of Crickhowell.

He needed a drink. He stopped off at The Dragon and rang The Gro. Martin said he'd walk down so he could have a proper drink. He stuck to his new regime and ordered a pint rather than his usual vodka tonic or wine. As he waited he couldn't help overhearing two men in their thirties who'd obviously had more than their fair share. They were agreeing that the most important thing in life was children - without them there was no point to life. Arwyn couldn't help thinking that if children were so important to them, why were they spending all their time in the pub. He went to sit as far away from them as possible.

He mulled over the talk he'd just had with his brother. He could see that he'd at last have to face up to his role in the debacle of their estrangement. For all these years, he'd been able to blame Bren without thinking too deeply about it. Even through he felt he could justify his actions, he realised now that that had been wrong.

It was with some relief that the door he was watching closely was thrust open and Martin marched in with his usual swagger. He went to the bar, ordered his pint and nodded towards Arwyn's to see if he wanted another, to which he readily greed.

'How was he tonight?' asked Martin, taking a seat next to him.'

'About the same. Quiet, but we had a good chat.'

Arwyn filled him in on what had been said, and his new thinking.

'Well, it was always a mystery to us,' said Martin, 'why you didn't speak and why it went on so long.

Bren would always clam up when I tried to broach the subject in a roundabout way. But after your wife was killed he did say he was hurt that you'd never brought her here.'

Diana was his second wife and the love of his life. He'd met his first, Samantha, at university and they'd married very young. Both started pushing their careers, she as a lecturer in International Relations, and worked long hours, hardly ever seeing each other. They drifted apart and were divorced inside three years. She went on to marry a Ghanaian and they set up a charity, building schools in West Africa. He married Diana, a barrister, a few years later and they were happy together for years until that terrible night when she was stabbed in their flat. The police said she must have walked in on burglars - there were two sets of strange fingerprints and the place had been ransacked. They'd never been caught. By that time his and Bren's distance was well established. He found solace in their friend Maxine and eventually they married, more for companionship than anything else. She'd died of cancer five years back.

Martin looked as if he was keeping something back, wondering whether or not to voice his thoughts.

'Bren did ask if I thought it was because Diana was black that you never brought her.'

'Good God, no.' Arwyn thought back. 'It never entered my mind, or hers, I'm sure. It just didn't happen, that's all.' But he had a nagging doubt that somewhere deep down there might have been a tiny element of that.

'And I was thinking,' continued Martin, 'that that was probably behind that bigot Ron Jones' attitude towards you. It was in the papers, you know, when she was killed. You being on the telly and all. There were pictures of her. Jones would have seen them, of course, and that's when he would have started that rumour that you killed her.'

'Well, well,' said Arwyn as he mulled this over.

'You should have brought her here, you know. That would have shown him. I've always wondered why she wasn't at your party.

'She was on a big trial and had to spend the weekend preparing her case. I told Bren about it at the time.'

'Well, another time then. And perhaps all this would never have happened.'

'Yes,' said Arwyn, nodding his head sorrowfully. 'Yes, I suppose you're right. We were always very competitive, so I suppose we were even vying for who could keep the silence up the longest. And as the weeks and months and years went on I suppose we became more entrenched, sure that the other was wrong. It's amazing what you can convince yourself of, given time.'

'It all seems a bit silly now, doesn't it?'

'Yes,' said Arwyn. 'It does.'

'You were always close, in your own way, weren't you?'

'In our own way. But I suppose part of being twins is asserting your own individuality, sooner or later, and when you're young that means putting the other one down in whatever way you can.'

He sipped his drink and thought back to their teen years. They'd long insisted their mother buy them different clothes. Up until the age of about fourteen it was Bren who'd been the most studious scholar. Then he found love with a girl of his own age who'd moved with her family from England. He began spending spent more time with his girlfriend than he did with books. Arwyn took over the baton and his place at the top of the class. If one showed an interest in something, the other would scoff at it. Bren started collecting birds' eggs, Arwyn took up the trumpet and joined the town band.

Arwyn told Martin he'd made up his mind to go back to London the next day. Martin gave what seemed to be a reproachful look but then shrugged. 'Well, if you've made your mind up…'

'I have. I've also thought that I've been taking up a lot of time with Bren, and he does get tired. Perhaps if I'm away for a few days it will encourage Jac to go in to see him. It would be nice if he did.'

Martin said he'd gone up to Jac's room that afternoon and found him gently sobbing to himself. Jac had merely said he was sad about Dad and would like to see him again soon so maybe he was indeed coming to terms with it in his own way. Arwyn nodded and hoped it would be so.

'I can see you need to sort out your own medicine,' said Martin. 'But have you thought about if…..' His voice trailed off.

'Yes, I have thought about it,' said Arwyn. 'And obviously the last thing I want is history repeating itself with what happened to our mother. But there's no telling when the end will come. He could go on for weeks or months, Martin, and let's hope he does. In a way. He himself, I think, is ready to go. He doesn't see much point in drawing it out, him lying there. So it's much better that I go now, and come back in a few days.'

'Well, if you're sure.'

'I'm not really sure,' said Arwyn. 'But I've made up my mind to go.'

13 Quartets of Ice Cream

The parting was painful at The Gro the next morning. Even though they'd explained to Jac that Arwyn would only be gone a few days to get his medicine, Jac hugged him on the doorstep as if he'd never let him go. Arwyn could see his nephew's eyes shining with tears and could feel his own welling up as he stroked his head. Arwyn realised, perhaps a little too late, that his departure would be another blow for Jac who was already missing his father.

'I don't want you to go,' said Jac.

'Neither do I,' said Arwyn, not wholly truthfully. 'But I've got to get my pills and I promise I'll come back as soon as I can.'

'Alright then,' he said, and loosened his hold so that Arwyn could gently disentangle himself.

He threw his rucksack in the back seat and climbed in beside Martin, waving at Jac and Sioned at the door. He was relieved to see Jac grinning broadly: he could recover his composure remarkably quickly.

Martin had insisted on driving him down to Newport so he could get a direct train to London. He'd suggested dropping by at St Winifred's so he could say ta-ta to Bren and tell him he'd be back soon, but Arwyn thought they'd both appreciate a clean getaway: neither could stand lingering goodbyes.

At the station he remembered to tell Martin about the shaving and gave him precise instructions. He'd left the kit in his bedroom. He was to put a hot flannel over his face for a few minutes, then apply a good dollop of moisturiser, then the shaving gel and the vibrating razor. Martin's eyebrows had risen at the mention of the moisturiser, but Arwyn said, 'It's how he likes it now. It's part of the ritual.'

After Martin had sped off, Arwyn noticed a poster announcing first-class upgrades for just a few pounds, and he thought he'd indulge himself. Why not, at his age? He settled down in his plush leather seat and couldn't help a smile of satisfaction playing on his lips. He did feel a sense of release in some ways, and was looking forward to being back in his flat where he had only himself to please. He told himself he was doing the right thing in going back, the thing he had to do to get his prescription, but his self answered back that he would have to face the consequences if something should happen.

As they neared the capital, he reflected that he was exchanging the fresh air of the Black Mountains for London's refreshing outlook on life, and was glad. He got a taxi from Paddington, and even the cheeky Cockney cabbie was a source of cheer. He let out a long sigh when he flung his backpack off in the flat, switched on the lamps - he hated the glaring ceiling lighting he'd had to endure for the past week - and surveyed his domain with satisfaction: the books, the pictures, the plants. He went into the kitchen to mix his drink and sunk into his leather chair, switching on Radio 3.

When he'd summoned the strength he rang The Gro as promised to let them know he'd got back safe and sound. Not much had changed at St Winifred's - they'd been there that afternoon and much to everyone's relief Jac had gone along. No, said Martin, there was no cajoling. They told him they were both going, simply asked him if he wanted to come and he'd said OK. He'd been quiet in the room with Bren, but his faint smile told them that it was alright. Bren had been good with him, saying that he didn't know how long he'd be there, but it might be a very long time because he wasn't well. But he wasn't to worry - Martin and Sioned would always take care of him, whatever happened. Jac seemed to accept this and was happier afterwards. This was music to Arwyn's ears, but Martin had broken off his narrative - a pregnant pause, as the cliché would have it.

'And?' said Arwyn.

'Well, I didn't mean to mention this, but at that point Jac asked if you would always take care of him too. We didn't know what to say. Just looked at each other and so I just said, well, yes.'

'Good,' said Arwyn. 'And how did Jac react to that?'

'His smile got a little bigger,' said Martin.

It was later that afternoon that he got a phone call from Mark Arnold, one of the old producers of *In Like Flint*. The programme editor, Miranda, had been taken to hospital with a suspected stroke. Her cleaner had gone to her house and found her in a confused state, not making much sense, and not being able to hold anything in her right hand. She'd called the ambulance and they'd whisked her off. She was asking for Arwyn. As she was in the Middlesex where he could easily walk, Arwyn thought he'd have no choice but to go, although just at the moment he was getting a bit sick of all this illness and dying. There was a word of warning from Mark: Miranda seemed to have taken the view that she was being held prisoner against her will and that anyone who went in to see her and wouldn't take her home was deemed to be part of the conspiracy to keep her there. When one mutual friend - a very good friend to Miranda for many years -had had the impudence to suggest that the doctors knew what they were doing, she was told in no uncertain terms to leave. He himself had just been and had come away with a huge flea in his ear.

'You know what she's like,' said Mark, before ringing off.

Yes, I know what she's like, thought Arwyn as he made his way over to Goodge Street. Feisty, funny, didn't suffer fools gladly: in fact she suffered them with the utmost disdain. She spoke her mind and a great mind it was. She was a wonderful boss - instinctive, decisive and supportive when she'd decided you were worth it.

He rang her mobile, not knowing what to expect. In his experience, strokes could have strange effects. One old colleague had come round speaking with a Scottish accent and fluent French.

'Oh A,' she said when she heard his voice. He was heartened that she recognised him and remembered her old moniker for him, claiming not be able to pronounce his name.

'It's awful. I'm just lying here being overlooked.'

He couldn't decide whether she meant ignored, checked over or stared at by other patients so merely informed her that he would come round that evening.

He found her sitting on the bed in a four-berth ward in the Buddha position wearing some kind of leotard. She didn't look particularly pleased to see him: it was as if he'd just walked in from the next room.

'Why are you late?' she demanded.

As no time had been mentioned, Arwyn ignored the question and asked her how she was. She started issuing instructions in a conspiratorial stage whisper.

'The......man in the white coat is coming soon. He's called Arwyn. I've told him you're here. You must get me out. I mean - look at them.'

She waved her arm imperiously around the other three beds in the ward. There was a Turkish woman in the corner who'd lost all mobility and been there two years (her three year-old daughter had known nothing else, according to Miranda); the elderly woman opposite her who slept all day (it's the drink, said Miranda, but she must have meant drugs) and the new occupant 'across the road' who she believed was Polish and 'a Jew.' She mouthed the word, and Arwyn wondered why: surely the stroke couldn't have rendered her racist. It was very unlike her.

The gist of her escape plan was that she'd done most of the required tests like showering herself and making a cup of coffee, and she'd been told she could leave the next night if she managed to walk up and down some steps and there was someone to stay the night with her. Her brother was coming over from Italy the day after, so she'd be fine.

'You just have to take me home. You don't have to stay the night - just tell them you're going to.'

At this, the doctor appeared, a youth called Alex. He asked Arwyn what he knew of Miranda's illness.

He summed up, mentioning her aphasia - impaired language due to brain damage - which he'd studied in Linguistics as part of his degree course. He had to keep telling Miranda not to interrupt.

Alex looked impressed, not to say alarmed, at this display of knowledge.

'And you'll take her home and stay with her for the first twenty-four hours, at least?'

'Yes,' said Arwyn firmly.

Alex looked him up and down as if wondering whether he could see himself home safely, let alone anyone else.

'The brain should repair itself in time, but she'll need speech therapy and aspirins.'

Miranda was now looking out of the window as if they were talking about someone else. Indeed, Nell had always taught her children that they should never say 'she' about someone who was in earshot. If they did, she would ask, 'Who's she? The cat's mother?'

After the doctor had gone, Miranda smiled for the first time.

'You needn't stay,' she said again.

'If I said I'll stay, I'll stay,' said Arwyn.

Mark rang the next morning to ask how the visit went. When Arwyn told him she was coming home, Mark sounded aggrieved, as if Arwyn was breaking ranks.

'Well, as long as you know what you're doing,' he said, sounding as if he very much doubted it.

He managed to get to the hospital on the dot of the appointed hour of four. Miranda was sitting in the bedside char with her coat on. He noticed that the bed across the room was empty too.

'Where's the Polish woman?'

'I had her removed,' said Miranda. Arwyn felt his stomach churn and wondered what on earth it could mean. It turned out that she'd been moved to intensive care. It was Miranda's little joke.

They got a cab to her house in Hampstead, Miranda giving clear instructions, Arwyn noted. He was encouraged by this, as he was still concerned about how she was going to cope. She was visibly delighted to be back home, and she looked more like her own self. He smiled as he watched her going around familiarising herself with things: brushing a side table with her fingertips, picking up an ornament from the bookshelf. The house was immaculate: Christine must have been in to clean.

When she was done, he was surprised to see her put her coat back on.

'I'm going to the.......place where the graves are,' she announced.

Arwyn asked her for details but did not elicit any more clarity. He assumed that she meant to go and see her parents in the nearby cemetery. He was on the point of insisting he went with her but then decided he had to see if she could take care of herself. When she'd gone he rang her brother Paolo to try to find out what time he'd be arriving the next day, but he was as vague as his sister: sometime in the afternoon. Arwyn explained that he had things to do and would have to leave about midday. Paolo said he must leave when he needed to and not to worry.

Miranda came home after about half an hour and seemed fine. She didn't offer any information about her outing and Arwyn didn't ask. She busied herself around the house and then went into the kitchen, getting out pans and food from the cupboard. He offered to help but she ignored him.

Mark rang Arwyn to ask how it all went, and he passed his phone over to Miranda. She seemed angry that Mark hadn't rung her and was curt with him.

By ten o'clock the meal was ready and they sat down at the kitchen table to eat it. It was slightly odd - chicken breast, omelette, rice and sliced tomatoes - but very welcome and Miranda had shown she could do it. She was tired now and started losing her words again.

'You know, Mark was quite nice when he came by himself. He used to bring me little quartets of...... olive oil.' She thought about it for a couple of seconds, and Arwyn waited.

'No - ice cream. Quartets of ice cream. Cartoons. Cartons. Cartons of ice cream.'

She seemed pleased when she finally got it and they both laughed.

'And a quarter of quarterbacks.'

Arwyn slept well in her neat and comfortable spare room. He went downstairs to find Miranda in the kitchen, a moka pot of coffee hissing on the stove. She was in a good mood. Arwyn made toast. She told him that Christine was coming today, but couldn't say what time, and that now she wanted to go shopping in Waitrose. Good, thought Arwyn - another skill he could tick off.

'Where is it?'

'There's one up there or one down there,' she said, not pointing in any direction. 'We have to drive to the one up there.' Arwyn wasn't sure about letting her drive, and it was as if she could sense his doubts.

'Let's walk,' she said, and they did.

The shopping went pretty well, except that she complained about the price of everything as if she hadn't been in a supermarket for years. She picked up a Gala melon and put it in the trolley.

'Right - now I need melons. Lemons.'

They got the bus back.

'You're so nice,' she said. 'Don't go,' and she laughed.

Christine was there when they got back and the women hugged like long lost friends. Arwyn tried to convey by looks to Christine that Miranda was OK. Christine smiled acknowledgement, and that she could see how much better Miranda was.

It was with some relief that Arwyn walked down to the tube station, but with a somewhat heavier heart. He'd sparred with Miranda for years, but he always admired her as a programme editor and they always got the best result in the end. They were a great team, and had a good laugh into the bargain. She was, he couldn't help feeling, diminished and he wondered what life would hold for her now. He could only hope that her brother would step up and help her. They'd never got on particularly well, but he was her only family and she'd managed to hack off most of her small coterie of loyal friends.

He felt worn out by all this illness, ageing and dying. He was badly in need of some light relief.

14.Klapperslanger

Steve had been a friend of Arwyn's since the Fleet Street days and rang him that afternoon.

'Hello, you old bugger. I'd given you up for dead.'

He always had that hail-fellow-well-met way of greeting, which Arwyn considered over the top. But now, in his dotage, he found him a real old fuss-pot, set in his ways, and, truth to tell, a bit of a snob. But if he found Steve's fussiness and fuddy-duddyness annoying, he reasoned to himself, Steve must surely find him lackadaisical. He tried to forgive him.

Arwyn summarised how he'd spent the last few days.

'What you need is to get out of yourself. How about supper at the Headline Club?'

That was what was needed, but somehow he couldn't drum up any enthusiasm for dining with his old friend. His conversation these days consisted mainly about the sick and the dying, and he just couldn't face it. Despite his many resolutions to be less grumpy with him, Arwyn seemed always to be a person he didn't like being when he was in his company. It was sad, but there it was. He didn't have the tolerance any more.

So he made his excuses, but when he'd put the phone down, he felt the evening stretching before him, and was sorry that he had. He'd got his pills, tidied up the flat, emptied the fridge and put out the rubbish. Even though he was dog tired, he wanted to do something, something he'd enjoy.

It was then, as if by some telepathy, that Freddie rang, unusually for him on a Thursday. His week-nights were usually spent in his family home in Beaconsfield, but occasionally he would spend a night or two in town, at a mystery location of course.

'I've tried you a couple of times in the last week or so,' he said, in tones that demanded an explanation.

Arwyn explained that the signals were bad in Wales, and that he had to go back the next day.

'How is your wombmate?' asked Freddie, and he smiled as he heard the old moniker for his twin. Freddie did have a way of lightening his mood.

'He could go any time,' said Arwyn.

'Well, how about a couple of drinks? I can tell that's what you need. I'm not far from you and can meet you in the Marylebone Tup in an hour. I'll make sure you don't overdo it.'

The pub was another of their old haunts - a typical old London one, with Victorian tiles, huge cut-glass mirrors and wooden booths. Arwyn made his slow way up Marylebone High Street but had left plenty of time so went to sit on a bench in the little park at Paddington Street. It was one of those oases in the middle of the hubbub. From the distance somewhere the faint strains of Amy Winehouse singing *Back to Black* reached him. On the opposite corner an old man with a fluffy grey beard was sitting on a camping stool playing his accordion, a hat on the ground in front of him. He must be Romanian, thought Arwyn, as most of the accordionists round there were. This was the hubbub that Arwyn loved. He marvelled that nine million people - three times the population of Wales - from so many cultures lived for the most part in harmony in this overcrowded city which had become his home. Of course there were problems, notably the tragic numbers of young black men who were stabbed to death in drug turf wars. Arwyn remembered doing a programme about it years ago, before it had reached the present-day devastating proportions. One of the most striking interviews was with a Reverend from the East End who worked tirelessly with gang members. In school they were told they were no good, he said, because maybe academically they weren't. So they decided if they couldn't be good, they would be bad - very bad. The conclusion of the programme was that the issue needed a holistic approach - education, training, youth programmes and so on. But here we were, years later, and it was getting worse.

Arwyn strolled over to the accordionist and dropped some change in his hat. They exchanged smiles. Another programme he'd done was on the psychology of giving. He often did give something to buskers because their music cheered him up. At a nearby bank there was a row of four cash machines, and people never knew whether to form one queue and hive off when a cashpoint became free, or to form separate queues behind each one. A young man with a sleeping bag and a dog was sitting on the ground shouting, 'Form one orderly queue please. Till number one please! Till number three please!' Arwyn gave him some money because he thought he was providing a useful service. Homeless charities' policy was not to give to people on the streets - there was shelter for people who were sober. Lately he'd taken to asking people outside supermarkets if they wanted a sandwich and he'd take them some fruit and water too. One guy had requested cheese and crackers, which Arwyn found amusing. He thought he'd better not get wine to go with it. But another time a young woman had approached him and said she wasn't going to lie, she was an alcoholic and needed money for booze. On an impulse he gave her some. He knew it was a stupid thing to do, but sometimes the heart rules the head.

He often bought a Big Issue as well, even though he thought the magazine could be much improved. He was walking to work one morning and a young man was standing a little further down the street with a copy in a plastic envelope.

He sang out, 'Here he comes! I know he's going to do it. I know he's going to buy a Big Issue.'

When Arwyn reached him, he gave him the money.

'You don't want this do you?' asked the man. 'It's my last copy.'

Arwyn laughed.

'Nah,' said the young man, 'it's all crap anyway.'

Freddie was sitting in one of the wooden booths with a bottle of red and two glasses when Arwyn arrived in the Marylebone Tup.

'Klapperslanger,' he said as he sat down, for no good reason that he could see.

Freddie poured him a glass and raised his. 'Klapper-slanger,' he said with a broad grin. 'Why do you say that?'

'Oh, I don't know. I've had a bit of week of it. I'm a bit under the weather, but you're right, this is what I need.'

'Let's 'wine' down,' said Freddie. 'And tell me about it.'

If there was one person he could tell, it was Freddie. And at last he could put some of his confused thoughts of the last few days into words.

'Don't be too hard on yourself,' said Freddie.

'I'm not, in a way,' said Arwwn. 'Charting your life ahead when you're young can be exciting but also daunting.......'

'I know all about that,' put in Freddie.

Arwyn remembered when he'd finally stirred himself from his drug den in the attic and joined the army. He'd sent Arwyn a card saying, "I couldn't have done it without you."

'But it's a mistake to try and chart your life back-wards,' he continued, 'all those what-ifs, that useless hand-wringing.'

He poured some water into his wine. The alcohol was helping him unburden himself but he knew he shouldn't overdo it.

'Yes, you have to face up to the consequences of your actions, and I think I've come to accept that. But my brother had a role to play in this strange silence too. We can't make up for lost time, but neither can we see these lost years as a total waste. That would be pointless too. It happened.'

'So you're going to go back?'

'Well, yes I have to. Especially after what happened to my mother. And I promised.'

'How long for?'

'Well that's the big question. It could be days, weeks, months. I'll have to make that decision later.'

'What did your nephew have to say about it?'

'He said there was a home there for me whenever I wanted it.'

He told him about Jones the Bigot, the gossip, the hostility.

'It's a weird place,' said Freddie.

Arwyn was about to continue with his thread but Freddie's words suddenly sunk in.

'Hang on. You never went there - well only once when you were tiny. You always wanted to when you were older, but never got it together.'

'Yes I did. I told you.'

'No you didn't. When?'

Freddie spent three or four years in the army and went on manoeuvres to the Brecon Beacons more than once. There was a training camp near Crickhowell. He now recounted that he wanted to see where his godfather had grown up - he'd always been fascinated with Arwyn's farm stories. He'd met Bren and Jac a couple of times when they came up to London and he'd hit it off with them and got Bren's number. There was even a running joke between Freddie and Arwyn about him going to live with Bren if ever he complained about anything in the flat in London.

Freddie said he had a day off when he was at Crickhowell and had given Bren a ring. Bren had come down to pick him up and had taken him to show him around the farm.

Arwyn couldn't remember Freddie telling him any of this - maybe he'd blanked it out, because he did believe that Freddie was telling the truth. He asked his godson when this was and worked out it would have been a couple of years after the party, when they'd stopped speaking.

'How did it go?'

'It was interesting to see the farm, and your brother was great - very kind. But I felt it was a wasn't a very friendly place, at least not to outsiders. People looked at me funny when I opened my mouth because of my accent.'

'Did he ask after me?'

'Yeah, just asked if you were doing OK.'

'So you didn't go into the fact that we hadn't been speaking for a couple of years? You knew about that, right?'

'Yeah, you'd told me. I did wonder before I rang him if I could do anything to smooth things over between you but he didn't seem to want to talk about it. Neither did you.'

'Each as stubborn as the other, I suppose. And you reckon you told me about this?'

'I told you about my visit to the farm, but you weren't interested.'

Freddie got up to go to the toilet, saying, 'I'll be back.'

Arwyn now cast his mind back to the times when Will used to bring Martin up to the Smithfield Show and stay in the flat in London. Bren came up with Jac a few times too, before all this happened. They were good times, when all three brothers got on well together, despite their different ways of life.

'You're not going to move back there, are you?' asked Freddie when he came back.

'No,' said Arwyn. 'It's been good to revisit my roots, my past and to make it up with Bren. It's made me think about things in a different light. But I couldn't go back there to live. London's where I've made my life, for good or ill.'

'As you make your bed, so you must lie in it. I remember when I was living in your attic at my lowest point, you insisted that I made my bed every morning when I got up. You said it was a good thing mentally, because you'd achieved something right at the start of the day.'

'The start of your day then was more often in the afternoon than the morning.'

'Yes, yes, alright. Things are different now.'

'I'm glad.'

'And I'm glad you're not going for good. I'd miss our meetings,' said Freddie.

But Arwyn had just a tiny niggling worry somewhere at the back of his mind. Despite everything he'd told Freddie, and Martin, and himself, was he in fact getting too old for London?

15.Saturdays are black or white

He was welcomed as a hero at The Gro, particularly from Jac who bounced up for a hug and followed him around like a puppy, bombarding him with questions about why he went away and how long he was going to stay. He felt more at ease coming back this time, more at home, as long as he stayed out of the village shop. After supper Martin suggested they went down to The Dragon for a couple of pints - Sioned was going to a whist drive. Arwyn was tempted, but said he didn't really feel up to it. Martin raised an eyebrow, but didn't say anything. He poured himself a whisky and made the cup of coffee that Arwyn wanted, and they sat chatting at the kitchen table. Martin said he'd been into the shop and had a word with Ron Jones, whom he called The Rudest Man in Wales. He'd told him to lay off with the gossip. He'd found out that he was going to retire and the shop would be up for sale. Maybe it wouldn't survive as the village shop, and that was just too bad: people did their big shops in supermarkets now and although it was another sign of a disappearing world, life is change.

'So he wasn't aggressive with you? Mary Upper Bryn said he had a terrible temper on him.'

'Well, I'm bigger than he is. Like all bullies, he's a coward deep down.'

It was decided that Arwyn would go in to see Bren the next afternoon. Martin warned that little by little he was going downhill. There was no new prognosis, but it was as if he was giving up the fight somehow.

On the way, he stopped at the cemetery at Crickhow-ell. He walked along the main path and came to a slope. At the top was where his family were buried below three old yew trees: simple granite slabs lined up in a row. He said hello to his brother Will, who'd helped bring up the twins - fed them when they were toddlers, scolded them when they were naughty and supported Arwyn when he told him he wanted to go to university. On his first visit back from London, Will gave him one of his bear hugs and asked 'What's it like?' Arwyn found it difficult to boil down into words, but Will pressed on with his questions. 'Hast 'ee done any drugs?' he asked, with genuine curiosity. At this point Arwyn managed to struggle free from his crushing hug. He said he'd had a spliff or two. 'What's it like? What's a spliff like?' Arwyn said it was just like having a few drinks, only not as good. It was a warm memory. To this day, he always had to choke back a tear whenever he heard *Danny Boy*. It was Will's favourite song and Arwyn could remember him signing it. And it came back to him, all of a whirl: the lines he'd carried them... where?... all these years.

Not in his heart, surely, because he felt it was giving up on him, all of a sudden. But those words, Will's words, he heard them now, as if he were singing them:

Tis I'll be here in sunshine or in shadow, Oh,
Danny boy, oh Danny boy, I love you so.

He said hello his to father and to his mother he said simply, 'Sorry, Mam' - not that he thought that she was looking down on him, but he felt the need to say it.

The walk up the slope had taken it out of him - age could creep up on you like that. He sat down on a bench until he had recovered his wits and thought about his family. He now realised that what he'd at first taken for Bren's unfriendliness was in fact due to how ill he was feeling. He'd come here demanding answers on his brother's deathbed when it was true what Bren said, that he was just as much to blame. He could see that now.

As Arwyn went into reception at St Winifred's, Shirley was coming out with her coat on. They exchanged warm smiles.

'I was hoping to see you here.'

'I'm going off shift now, but don't worry - the rest of the staff are almost as nice as me.'

'Martin says he's getting weaker.'

'He is. Maybe I shouldn't be saying this to you, but I think you should prepare yourself. You can see the doctor if you want.'

'Thanks, Shirley.' She

clasped his hand.

'Best of luck. To both of you.'

Arwyn did indeed find his brother thinner, greyer and weaker. But he looked pleased to see him and was eager for his shave. As he was lathering his stubble, Arwyn said, 'Martin says you're not fighting it any more.'

'Does he now?'

Arwyn wanted to get this over with before he started on the razor.

'Well, is it true?'

'I don't know Ar. It gets harder as you get weaker. Sometimes I feel like the cat that French minister called Brexit.....'

He took a couple of moments to catch his breath.

'…….because he would wait at the door to go out, but when it was opened he'd just sit there looking at the other side.'

Another pause, as Arwyn got out the razor.

'And it's easier with all this Brexit bollocks,' said Bren. 'I don't know what's happening to people. It's becoming the kind of country I don't want to live in any more.'

'I know. The world doesn't make much sense any more. You're supposed to get wiser as you get older, but more and more I find there aren't any answers to my questions.'

Arwyn started the shave, and realised he'd have to do the talking for a while. He said he'd heard Tony Benn's diaries on the radio, when he was reading about the end of his wife's life. It had been a long and painful illness, and one of the nurses suggested it might be easier if he told his wife she could go if she wanted to, so he did. And she died. He said afterwards that his wife taught him not to be afraid of death, to see it as an adventure. Like Baudelaire, thought Arwyn.

When he'd finished cleaning off the foam, he said down in the high-backed chair at the head of his brother's bed and asked, 'Is that what you want? Per- mission to go?'

'No. No, not really. I suppose I think you go when your time's up, and that's it.'

"Remember we used to argue about who would live the longest.'

'Well, it seems you're going to win that one,' said Bren, with what he had left of a chuckle.

'I don't know. Maybe it won't feel like the winner when I'm the only one left.'

'Perhaps not.'

'At least you know there's nothing to worry about. Martin will carry on the farm, Jac will be taken care of…..'

'Oh yes. I can't worry about Jac. You know, in the early days we'd take him to see all kinds of doctors and psychiatrists. One of the asked me if I'd ever thought, "Why me?"'

Bren paused for breath.

'And I said no, because I never had. Nor Meryl. Partly because there's no answer to that question, so there's no point in asking it. But also because, despite all the challenges, we saw Jac as a gift. He enriched our lives.'

'Yes, I can see that. I feel the same way myself.

Bren looked pleased.

'And what about you? What will you do? Go back to London?'

Arwyn supposed he would. He'd made his life there and had got used to being able to get on with it without being judged. He recounted the episode with Ron Jones at the shop, and asked Bren if he'd ever heard the rumour about him killing his wife.

'Good God, no. He'd have had me to answer to if I had. He was always a nasty bugger. No-one liked him. Perhaps that's what made him the way he was.'

There was certainly that side to rural life, said Bren. You had to take the rough with the smooth wherever you were. Arwyn had private doubts about that, but thought it wasn't the moment to voice them. There was another pause.

'Do you think Mam resented me going away?'

'No, she wanted you to. You were smart.'

'So were you.'

'In different ways, perhaps.'

'The same, but different.'

'Yes. What she did mind was you not coming back often enough.'

'Yes, well, we've been through that,' said Arwyn. 'I felt I had to get on with making my way in life. It's only later that these things seemed important.'

'They were important to her.'

'You know, I asked her once which of us she loved the most, and she gave what I thought was a good answer: whoever needs me most at the time.'

'Did I need her more than you?' mused Bren. 'Maybe. Stayed physically closer anyway. I always thought she would have gone away to university in a different world.'

'Yes, so did I. But then we might never have existed.'

'Doesn't bear thinking about.'

'No. I called at the cemetery on the way here, to see the graves.'

'Hmm - more than I've done recently, I must say.'

'And I said sorry to Mam.'

Bren nodded, as if to say good on you.

All those arguments they used to have, all those racing rivalries didn't seem to matter at all now, thought Arwyn. He reminded Bren of their futile debate over the colour of the days of the week. A few years before a radio producer friend of his was making a pro-

gramme about this rare phenomenon, called synaes-
thesia. You either had it or you didn't she'd said, and
it was unimaginable to those who didn't. She didn't.
She'd asked him if she could record his colours, so
he'd gone into a studio in London and spoke down the
line to Cardiff. After he'd finished, she said simply.
'Arwyn - you're mad.'

'I've forgotten yours,' said Arwyn.

'I haven't thought about this for years,' said Bren.

'Can you still see them?'

'Of course. Laid out side by side like those strips of
paint colours.'

'Yes, that's how I see them. OK, let's do it.'

'Do what?'

'List our colours. We don't have to argue about them
now. It's just what we see. I'll go first. Monday is
royal blue.'

For a moment Bren looked as if he too thought Arwyn was mad and that he certainly wasn't going to
join in. But then he said with a sigh: 'Monday is light
blue.'

'OK, at least we're not totally at odds over Mondays.'

'Get on with it. I haven't got all day.'

'Tuesdays are primrose yellow.'

'Tuesdays are orangey - or ochre, is it?'

'Wednesdays are red.'

'Tsk. Wednesdays are green.'

'Thursdays are grey, and in the middle is that little symbol for a marsh that you see on maps.'

'Thursdays are blue-grey.'

'Fridays are off-white.'

'Fridays are brown.'

'Saturdays are black.'

'Saturdays are white.'

'Hmm.'

'And Sundays? What comes next?' Bren had a vaguely sardonic look on his face. What indeed comes next?

'Sundays are sandpaper.'

'Sandpaper isn't a colour.'

'It's what I see. That producer told me that someone she read about had Sundays as stainless steel.' 'Sundays are charcoal.'

There was another silence, as Bren now seemed exhausted. It was companionable and peaceful. Arwyn thought he should go, but he too was tired.

After a while, he sensed Bren stirring, and he gave him some water.

'Did you resent me going away?'

'No. You always looked outward. I knew you would.'

'You seemed to have a right cob on the day I left.'

'I didn't want to see you go. But eighteen year-old boys can't express that. Or at least we couldn't, then. So I kept out of the way.'

The light was fading. A nurse came in to ask if they were both OK.

'Yes. I won't be long now.' said Arwyn.

'Take as long as you like,' said the nurse with a kind smile.

'So you have no real regrets?' Arwyn asked his brother.

'No big ones. No time for 'em. We were lucky,' said Bren. 'We lived our own lives.'

'Yes,' said Arwyn. 'We lived our own lives.'

For a long while, the brothers didn't speak. Bren seemed to be drifting off. Eventually his heart monitor became one long line. But Arwyn didn't see it. His eyes had closed.

Printed in Great Britain
by Amazon